REVOLUTION: A FOUR WORLDS STORY

SKYLER RAMIREZ

Copyright 2024, Skyler S. Ramirez

All rights reserved

The characters and events portrayed in this book are fictitious. Any similarity to real persons, living or dead, is coincidental and not intended by the author.

No part of this book may be reproduced, or stored in a retrieval system, or transmitted in any form or by any means, electronic, mechanical, photocopying, recording, or otherwise, without express written permission of the publisher.

Cover design by: Juan Padrón

Published by: Persephone Entertainment Inc.

Texas, USA

Printed in the United States of America

Dedicated to the fans of The Four Worlds series. Enjoy this deeper look into the universe!

Don't ever miss a new release!

Sign up now for Skyler's newsletter and get access to new release updates, free content, and great deals.

Just go to www.skylerramirez.com/join-the-club

CONTENTS

Map of Human Space — ix
Preface & Recap of Important Concepts Prior to Reading — xi
Dramatis Personae — xv

PART ONE
FENG

1. Career Day — 3
2. Training — 9
3. Running the Course — 21
4. Playing in the Park — 27
5. Deployment Orders — 33
6. Revelations — 37
7. Death Valley — 45
8. Sacrifice — 49
9. Recordings — 57
10. Deserter — 61

PART TWO
PATEL

11. Trial — 71
12. The Asteroid — 75
13. Roommates — 81

PART THREE
TREASONOUS BEGINNINGS

14. Rebel Emissary — 91
15. Friendly Fire — 97
16. Mech Down — 101
17. Brick Wall — 105
18. Sabotage — 113
19. Revenge — 115
20. Collateral Damage — 117
21. Plan of Attack — 121
22. Escalation — 125
23. Headache — 129
24. Brick Wall Revisited — 133

25. Beating	137
26. Jungle Trek	145
27. Accidental Murder	151
28. Messenger	157
29. Death from Above	161
30. Volunteers	169
31. Stockade	171

PART FOUR
ENDGAME

32. March	177
33. Base	179
34. Attack	183
35. Broadcast	189
36. Treason	197

PART FIVE
AFTERMATH

37. Admiral	207
38. Rebel	211
Epilogue	215
Books by Skyler Ramirez	219
About the Author	223

Map of Human Space, Circa 700 P.D.

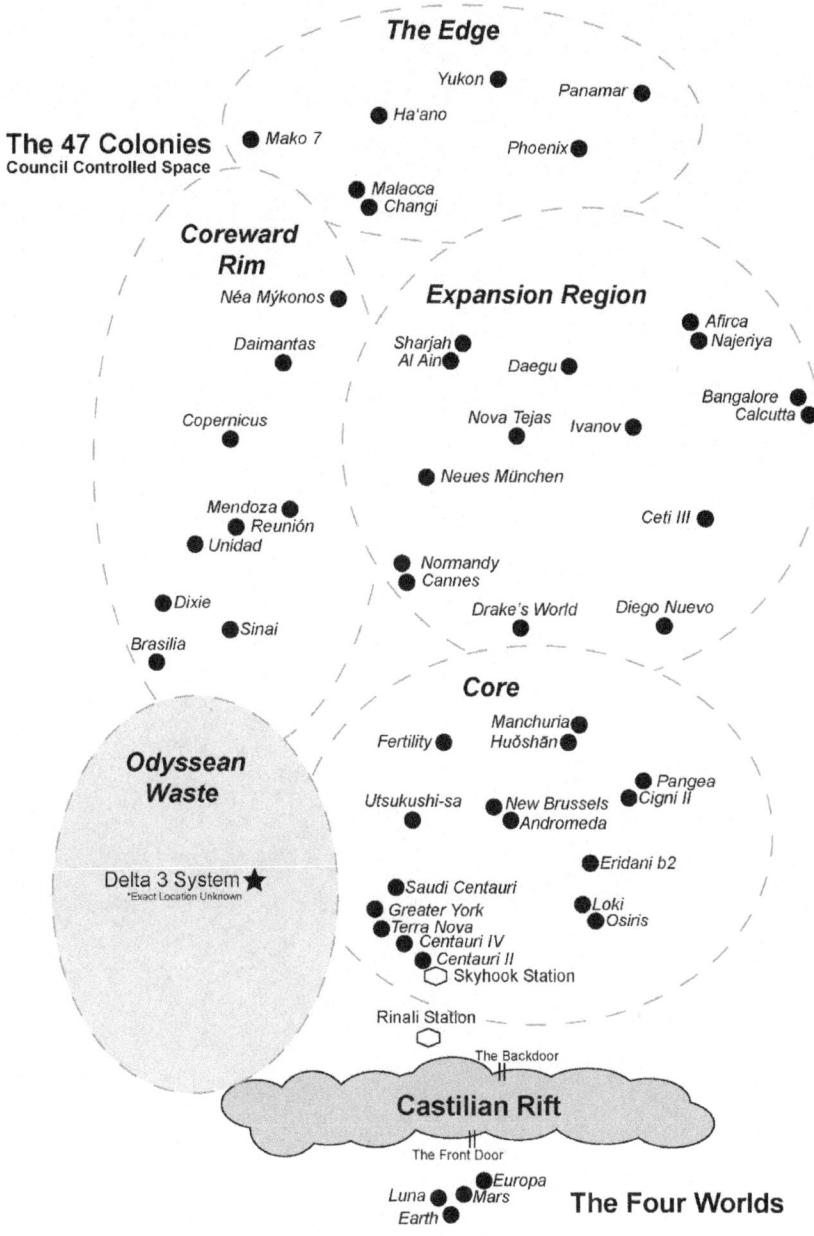

PREFACE & RECAP OF IMPORTANT CONCEPTS PRIOR TO READING

Revolution – A Four Worlds Story is a side novel set in the universe of *The Four Worlds* series. As such, much of the story that follows will not make sense without the context of the first two books in that series (*The Four Worlds: The Truth* and *The Four Worlds: Subversion*). If you haven't already read those two books, I would recommend doing so first. If it's been a while, I would recommend re-reading the prologue to *The Four Worlds: Subversion*, which is really the start of this story.

However, for those who choose to instead start their journey with this book or who need a refresher on the series before proceeding, I've included some of the basic concepts below to enhance your enjoyment of this novel:

The Council: The Council is the government of the 47 Colonies of Humanity. The Council controls everything for the good of humanity and is supposedly made up of the brightest and most virtuous men and women in the galaxy for each generation. In order to maintain themselves separate from politics and public opinion, members of the Council are anonymous and speak to the people only through the Keeper, who is the head of the Assembly.

In reality, the Council is a lie. Hundreds of years ago, a corrupt Keeper had all members of the Council killed, and since then, the

Keepers, plus a small number of senior Assembly members, have been the true rulers of the 47 Colonies.

The Assembly: A legislative body that supposedly helps the Council rule the 47 Colonies. The Assembly includes representatives of each and every colony, though representation is weighted heavily toward the more populated Core worlds. Members of the Assembly must be speakers (see 'The Enhanced' below).

The Enhanced: Genetically enhanced individuals who are the descendants of men and women long ago engineered by the Council to serve its needs. All enhanced individuals fall into one of four categories: Enacters, Speakers, Readers, or Blenders. This book will deal only with Enacters.

Enacters: Enhanced individuals genetically engineered to be perfectly obedient to a single authority for their entire lives. Enacters imprint upon the principal authority figure in their lives around the age of six. All enacters in the 47 Colonies are taken from their families at the age of five and indoctrinated in Enacter Academies, where they are taught that the Council is the sole legitimate authority figure in the galaxy. Parents are allowed no contact with their children from that time forward in life. This virtually guarantees that all enacter children imprint on the Council. The Council then uses its enacters to fill top law enforcement and other government positions.

Because enacters receive their orders from the Council via the Keeper and the chain of command, they are truly controlled by the Keeper and his cronies.

Enacters who try to disobey orders from the Council (Keeper) or its duly-appointed representatives experience intense pain brought on by their genetic mutation. Those few who attempt to fight through the pain usually lose consciousness, whereupon their subconscious takes over and attempts to halt the agony by forcing them to comply with the Council's orders.

In the history of the 47 Colonies, there is only one recorded instance of an enacter ever successfully disobeying the Council. That enacter was Tyrus Tyne (a main character in *The Four Worlds* series).

However, there are rumors of other enacters who have also failed to obey perfectly. And it is a closely-held secret within the government that the genetic bloodlines for the enhanced have been weakening, leading to more and more instances of disobedient enacters.

The Guard: The police force for all of the 47 Colonies. Open to all, but run exclusively by enacters in the upper ranks. It is technically a civilian organization since the Council has no official military. However, the Guard Space Force (GSF) and Guard Paramilitary Force (GPF) serve as its paramilitary arms.

The Revelations: In 731 P.D. (post Diaspora), a rogue senior member of the Assembly (and secret rebel leader), Kendra Siefred, released a series of damning claims about the Council to the public. In these so-called 'Revelations', she revealed the truth about the Council and the Keeper. She also revealed the truth about Tyrus Tyne's disobedience, giving hope to other enacters across the galaxy.

One of the most damning of the Revelations, however, was Siefred's claim (supported by proof supplied by Jinny Ambrosa, Alan Daily, and Tyrus Tyne, main characters in *The Four Worlds*) that the Keeper has been poisoning food and water supplies across the colonies in an effort to change the entire populace into enacters to secure his rule and reinvigorate the failing bloodlines of the Enhanced.

The Revelations have been used by some small groups within the 47 Colonies to justify open rebellion against the Council. This story deals with one such rebellion on the planet Panamar.

Panamar: A small colony planet in the Fringe, the area of space furthest from the Core worlds. Panamar has often been the location of insurrection and opposition to Council rule. The people of Panamar, supported by Siefred's rebel forces, have used the Revelations as a reason to rise up in rebellion yet again. This is where our story primarily takes place.

DRAMATIS PERSONAE

GPF (GUARD PARAMILITARY FORCE)

Private Feng Chu Hua – *Female.* Enacter and mech driver in the GPF, sent to Panamar to suppress the rebellion there. Gifted mech driver and standout performer in her unit.
Sergeant Sarah Nowak – *Female.* Enacter and mech driver in the GPF. Private Feng's superior. New mother, ending her maternity leave early to deploy to Panamar with her unit.
Captain Bohdi Patel – *Male.* Non-enacter officer in the GPF infantry. Pressed into GPF service to avoid a prison sentence but quickly rose through the ranks based on intelligence and merit.
Lieutenant Jose Sandoval – *Male.* Enacter officer in the GPF mechanized division. Superior to both Sarah Nowak and Feng Chu Hua. Former roommate to Bohdi Patel. A lackluster officer, too rigid in his thinking to be promoted.
Major Tiffany Rodriguez – *Female.* Non-enacter officer in the GPF infantry. Bohdi Patel's superior and secret girlfriend. Has risen to the maximum rank a non-enacter can obtain in the GPF.
Captain Kimberley Portenoy – *Female.* Non-enacter officer in the GPF infantry.

GSF (GUARD SPACE FORCE)

Sub-Commander George Cornwall – Executive officer on the Guard Heavy Cruiser *Solstice*, in orbit around Panamar. An enacter.
Sub-Commander Rory Lang – Chief engineer on the Guard Heavy Cruiser *Solstice*, in orbit around Panamar. A non-enacter.

FCN (FREE COLONIES NAVY)

Lt. Commander Xin Wang – *Male*. Fighter pilot and squadron leader in the rebel navy. Sent by the leader of the rebel military, Admiral Gerald Williams, to serve as his liaison to the rebel ground forces on Panamar.
Admiral Gerald Williams – *Male*. Supreme military leader of the Free Colonies rebellion, serving under the civilian leadership of Kendra Siefred prior to her death. His civilian cover is as the merchant captain of the freighter *Lucille*, which is really a heavily armed battlecruiser in disguise. Responsible for helping Jinny Ambrosa, Alan Daily, and Tyrus Tyne (main characters from *The Four Worlds*) escape the Council.

FCA (FREE COLONIES ARMY)

Colonel Sam Kilgore – *Male*. Special forces leader in the rebel ground forces on Panamar. Has been fighting the Council and the Guard most of his life via guerrilla warfare.
General Juan Bolivar – *Male*. The leader of the rebel ground forces on Panamar. Was a commander of a Guard Special Tactics (GST) team on the planet, and had risen as high as he could in the ranks as a non-enacter. Secret rebel sympathizer most of his life, he publicly left the Guard and took command of the FCA forces when open rebellion broke out on Panamar.

There are other minor characters, not listed here, that come into and out of the story at various points as well.

PART ONE
FENG

ONE
CAREER DAY
FENG CHU HUA

THREE YEARS AGO – 728 P.D. (POST DIASPORA)

"Oooh, the Prefecture is hiring!" Joanna Moss almost squealed in delight and started heading toward the largest booth at the Enacter Academy job fair. Feng Chu Hua rolled her eyes but let her roommate pull her by the hand behind her.

When the two eighteen-year-old girls reached the booth, a man with a shiny business suit and a smooth, overly polished voice—he had to be a speaker—was regaling a large group of their fellow graduating classmates about the virtues of working for the Greater York planetary government.

"We have openings in the Department of Weights and Measures, the Department of Water, the Bureau of Land Management, and the Department of Sanitation. A career with the Planetary Prefecture guarantees your growth as a servant of the Council and provides numerous opportunities to..."

Chu Hua tuned the man out as he droned on about all the wonderful benefits of becoming a faceless bureaucrat. Her eyes wandered around the spacious hall in which the career fair was being hosted for all the graduating students of the class of 728 P.D. There were depressingly few booths. Enacters only had so many career paths they could choose from, and not all of those had openings every year. The Enacter Academy at least made an effort to allow the students to self-select into the available postings. But when that didn't work, they simply ordered the graduating students to fill any remaining gaps.

It wasn't like the students could say no.

Chu Hua had come to grips with her fate as an enacter long ago. Ripped from her parents at the tender age of five, indoctrinated in the Enacter Academy to ensure she imprinted on the Council and taught from then onward that her life would be in service to the same, she had long ago given up wondering what life as a non-enacter might be like.

But that didn't mean she had given up on any semblance of excitement in her life. And now, listening to the representative of the Planetary Prefecture drone on about wonderful opportunities in water and sanitation, she felt a depression start to settle over her. Maybe Joanna could get excited about administrating the fourth water district's algae levels in the hopes of one day earning a more prestigious post as chief dog catcher or something like that, but not her. There was only one booth in the entire hall that interested Feng Chu Hua.

And it was right there, just twenty meters away, with a shiny gold shield the size of a Mendozan Bearcat hanging from the ceiling to draw attention. She looked over at Joanna, who was completely under the speaker's spell, engrossed in his description of administering land-use policies in Greater York's southern hemisphere. She didn't even notice her roommate leaving as Chu Hua made her way over to the other booth.

In front of the booth, a tall man in a trim blue dress uniform stood with his back straight and an intense gaze directed at every student who passed by. His eyes locked on Chu Hua when she was still ten meters away. But instead of interest, his gaze conveyed only an amused disdain. Still, she squared her shoulders and moved right on up to the man, looking up from her diminutive 1.4-meter height, which effectively had her staring at the hairs in his nose. But she put all the conviction she could into her voice.

"I'd like to join the Guard."

The man regarded her, his mouth twitching up in one corner. To his credit, at least he didn't break out laughing. But he did shake his head. "Listen, I'm sure you do. There is no greater honor than protecting the galaxy and the peace and order the Council brings. But, no offense, you're just not what we're looking for."

Feng's heart sank. His response wasn't unexpected, but actually hearing the words crushed a hope that she had held inside her since she was seven years old, and her Academy class had watched a vid on the role of the Guard in safeguarding the peace and the Council's will in the 47 Colonies. Ever since that day, Chu Hua had harbored only one career aspiration. And it had just died with a whimper.

"Please," she said. "I need to join the Guard. I would make an excellent guardswoman." She knew that her preternaturally high-pitched voice didn't convey the depth of emotion she felt, nor did it impart the confidence she was trying to project. But she could only work with the tools she had.

The man frowned and shook his head again. "Listen, kid. The Guard may look like a whole lot of spit and polish and parades, but it's a difficult assignment. If you can't run down a hundred-kilo perp and wrestle him to the ground, then you'll only be putting yourself and your fellow guardmembers in danger. Kudos to you for wanting to do something noble, but maybe the Engineering Corps would be a better fit for you. They're always looking for people who can fit into small spaces." He shrugged and turned away, clearly expecting the conversation to be over.

But Chu Hua wasn't ready to give up. If the man ordered her to leave him alone, she would have no choice. Even though he wasn't her immediate superior, he still spoke for the Council as a Guard officer, which meant she would be compelled to obey him by that nasty part of her genetics and her subconscious mind that demanded perfect obedience to the government. But he hadn't given her an order yet.

She put a hand on his arm, and he looked down in surprise that she was still there. "What about the Space Force?" she asked. "Don't they need engineers who can fit into small spaces too?" It was a last-ditch attempt, and she knew it. But she needed to be a guardswoman. If she had to work for the Department of Sanitation...

The officer sighed and gave her a sympathetic look. "It doesn't work that way. The Space Force isn't a separate entity. Everyone starts out as a regular guardmember planetside, patrolling the streets. After a few years of that, you can apply to a rotation with the Space Force and even possibly do the rest of your career there. But if you can't do the job of enforcing the laws on the streets, you'll never make it that far. And you don't meet the minimum physical requirements. Giving you a slot would only be setting you up for failure, and it would take away a spot from someone else with a real chance of making it. I'm sorry."

Chu Hua felt her eyes growing hot with nascent tears, but she tried to remain stoic. "Thank you for your time," she said in almost a whisper, and then she turned and moved away from the booth as quickly as she could before the floodgates broke. She didn't need the final humiliation of the man seeing her cry.

"Hey, you there, wait!" a rough feminine voice called out from behind her, but Feng kept walking, trying to remember where the closest bathroom was so she could lock herself in a stall and be alone for a few precious moments to compose herself. She needed to mourn the death of her dream before she had the courage to go find her consolation career elsewhere.

But a hand grabbed her by the shoulder and physically pulled her to a stop. "I said, wait!" the same voice called, now almost directly in her ear.

Chu Hua spun around, automatically looking up to see who had accosted her—she was used to everyone being taller than her. But she was surprised to see a woman's face that was only a few centimeters higher than her own. Like the man at the Guard booth, she wore a blue dress uniform, but the cut and style were different, reminding Feng of a holo vid she'd once seen of an ancient homeworld military fighting off anti-Council forces before the plague that destroyed Earth.

"Are you crying?" the woman asked incredulously.

Feng tried desperately to hide her face by looking down and then quickly wiping her tears on her sleeve, but she knew she was fooling no one. She braced herself for the disdainful comment that was sure to come next. But unexpectedly, the woman smiled. "Wow, you must really want to be in the Guard. What's your name, Enacter Trainee?"

"Enacter Trainee Feng Chu Hua, from Huoshan, ma'am."

"OK, Feng Chu Hua from Huoshan. Why do you want to join the Guard?"

Feng looked at the woman in confused silence. Was she rubbing the rejection in? Did she have no compassion at all? But at least the answer was one that Chu Hua had rehearsed a dozen times in the mirror, even though she hadn't even had a chance to give it to the dismissive Guardsman at the booth.

"To maintain peace and order in the galaxy, ma'am. To fight against those who defy the Council and put their fellow citizens at risk. To make the 47 Colonies safe for all the Council's children."

The woman frowned, which wasn't the reaction Feng had been expecting at all! "Really?" she asked in a flat tone. "That sounds like a line from a recruiting vid. I didn't ask for that. I asked why *you* want to join the Guard."

Taken aback, Feng struggled to think and form the words. A dozen possible responses flit through her mind, but nothing stuck. She had no idea what this woman wanted to hear or even why. She'd already been rejected. Finally, figuring she had nothing to lose at this point, she answered as honestly as she could.

"I really don't want to monitor algae levels for the Department of Water for the rest of my life, ma'am. I'll go mad. I need something that makes me feel like I matter."

It was a silly response, a stupid response, and Chu Hua felt the blood rushing to her face as her ears burned in embarrassment.

But the woman surprised her again, breaking out into a wide grin. "Now, that's more like it, Feng Chu Hua from Huoshan. Tell me, have you ever heard of the Guard Paramilitary Force?"

Feng frowned. She had heard of the paramilitary force, of course, but never even considered it as a potential career path. The GPF was small compared to the Guard overall and was best known as a place for the dregs of society to go. Steal a hovercar? Choose between ten years in prison or five years in the GPF fighting farmers with pitchforks who didn't want to pay their taxes on Malacca or suppressing riots at food distribution points on Afirca or Calcutta. No one wanted to join the paramilitary forces. So why was a recruiter at an Enacter Academy career fair even asking her about them?

"Of course," she said slowly, not managing to keep the uncertainty from her tone.

The other woman only smiled wider, and her eyes twinkled with mirth. "Don't believe everything you hear, kid. The GPF is much more than you think. There are two whole divisions made up entirely of enacters. Why? Because we can't trust anyone else with the kind of firepower we wield in defense of the Council and the colonies. Interested?"

Feng looked at her now with confusion. Hadn't she already been told there was no hope for her with the Guard? A hundred questions almost rose to her lips, but what came out was far simpler and surprising even to her. Because she really didn't want to work with algae in the hopes of one day being promoted to head water tester or some other soul-sucking job where all she did was follow the orders of other enacters with no original thought of her own. "Yes. I'm interested."

The woman slapped her on the shoulder and nodded. "Good. Listen, Feng Chu Hua, have you ever seen a mech?"

Chu Hua shook her head dumbly in response.

"Terrible things," the woman said, leaning in conspiratorially. "They're hot and stuffy, and one wrong move can bring down a building if you don't know what you're doing. They're also huge on the outside but way too small on the inside. Practically have to be rail thin to even fit in one of the blasted things. And you have to be pretty short, too."

She paused, regarding Feng with mock seriousness. "Say, Feng Chu Hua of Huoshan, you look short and skinny. I think you'd fit into a mech quite nicely. May even have some room to spare. And it just so happens that I'm here recruiting for a few spots in one of those big, smelly mechs. What a fortuitous meeting this is!"

Feng allowed the woman to guide her to a small booth next to the larger Guard booth, with a much smaller silver shield hanging above it that couldn't compete with the gold monstrosity that hung over the booth next door. But there, she told Feng all about how her life was going to change forever.

TWO
TRAINING
CADET FENG CHU HUA, GPF

EIGHTEEN MONTHS AGO – 729 P.D.

"Sprite, on your left!"

Feng Chu Hua—she hated it when people called her Sprite—jammed her right leg down, hard, to create a pivot point and used the momentum of her ton-and-a-half training mech to spin around that point and redirect her suit on a perpendicular course. That alone kept her from being hit in the back by the two dummy missiles launched from the mech behind her.

That was way too close, she thought in anger as her mech suit screamed a proximity alarm at her. The missiles themselves were almost too fast for her to see as they streaked past, but the suit could see them, and it wasn't happy about how narrowly they missed impacting her back.

Ahead, the target—the target Feng had been aiming for—turned from red to gray as the dummy missiles hit, and the exercise AI deemed that the target had been destroyed.

Chu Hua swore as Trey Parkins laughed through the direct comm link with her suit. The blasted borzak had done that on purpose! He'd known that Chu Hua was going for that same target. Not only had he taken out her target, but he'd barely warned her in time to prevent a friendly fire incident. And now he was laughing about it!

"What's wrong, Sprite?" he asked in a mocking tone. "Are you upset that I'm going to beat you again?"

"In your dreams, Parakeet," she said back, wishing her almost preternaturally high soprano voice could sound meaner. But at least it shut him up. She'd taken to calling him 'Parakeet' just a few days after he and others had started calling her 'Sprite', and if she hated her nickname, he loathed the one she'd chosen for him. Feng loved that it was actually catching on, and some of the other students were starting to call him that, too.

She cut the comm channel before he could think of another snide response and checked her suit heads-up display for her next target. That's when she saw it: a big red flashing light right in the center of the exercise field, a light that hadn't been there just a few seconds before.

Chu Hua smiled wickedly to herself. It was the boss.

The official name for it was the primary target, but all of the cadets at the Guard Mechanized Warfare School called it the 'boss' for reasons that had never made sense to Chu Hua. She'd heard it had something to do with video games, but most of them had never even played a video game—they weren't exactly part of the curriculum at the Enacter Academy. Still, no matter what it was called, the 'boss' was the target to end all targets, worth quadruple points to anyone who took it out.

Of course, it carried such a high point score because it was also so much harder to take out, usually surrounded by cover and itself heavily armed. And the boss wasn't a stationary target like the others; it could move and fight back.

She ran in its direction now, watching as the other green dots on her HUD, her classmates, also converged toward the flashing red dot. She smiled, seeing that she had a head start on all but one of them: Parkins.

Her comm signaled an incoming message from the man, no doubt to gloat that he was twenty meters ahead of her on his way to take out the boss. She ignored it. Parakeet was fast; Chu Hua was faster.

For this exercise, they were in an urban setting. It wasn't always like that; the exercise field changed every week. Last week, it had been mountain terrain; the week before that, a coastal village. But now, it reminded her vaguely of Shining Rain, the biggest city closest to her parents' village on her home planet of Huoshan. Of course, she hadn't seen her parents or their village since the age of five, when she'd been taken away from them to attend the Enacter Academy on Greater York. But she'd spent some time touring the area virtually, wanting to feel some connection to her roots.

Now, she ran as quickly as she could down the narrow city streets toward what looked like a large bombed-out building that could have once been a sports arena. It was the only part of the mock city that looked as if it had already been host to a major battle, and she had avoided it up until this point, as it had seemingly housed no targets.

She saw Parakeet sprinting his mech still about twenty meters in front of her. She knew she could make her mech run faster than his, so she poured on the speed, finding the easy rhythm that oddly came naturally to her and not to most of the other cadets. It allowed her training mech to reach just over its supposed top-rated speed. Her instructors hadn't believed it was possible the first time she'd done it, but when she'd done it the second and then the third time, they'd finally had to admit that it wasn't a problem with their sensors. Not even she could quite explain how she did it, only that there was a certain sequence of movements between her arms and legs at a cadence that she could simply feel that propelled her mech forward in a way that the designers had never intended but that made it go fast.

Stopping, however, was another issue entirely. As she rounded a corner behind Parakeet, she saw the traffic barricade in front of her, blocking half the road. Parkins had gone around it, but she didn't react in time, instead trying to stop her mech's forward run...unsuccessfully. She knew how to get herself into the right rhythm to run her mech above its top speed, but getting out of that rhythm always proved awkward.

She hit the barricade going close to 50 km/h, her legs and arms flailing as she clumsily tried to stop in time. The concrete barrier only came up to her mech's knees, but it was enough to trip her and send the massive machine tumbling end over end, spinning her inside the cockpit and sending her HUD into a paranoid series of queries and menus opening and closing as it tried to make sense of her facial movements as commands.

It took her a second to get the mech back on its feet, and she got up just in time to see Parakeet round another corner 30 meters ahead. All the ground she'd begun to gain was gone, and then some. Swearing, Chu Hua started running the mech again, but it took her longer to shake off the shock of the fall and get back into her rhythm. By the time she did so, Parkins was 40 meters ahead, and they were now only half a kilometer from the primary target. Even with her superior running speed, Chu Hua knew she'd never catch up...unless she did something drastic.

As she finally rounded the corner behind Parkins, she saw they were now on a broad avenue that led straight to the bombed-out arena where their target waited. Her HUD showed no one else as close as her and Parkins, but he was far enough ahead that not even the straight-away would allow her to close the distance.

Staying in her space-eating rhythm, she twitched her left eye to cause her HUD to zoom in on the arena in front of her and Parakeet. Despite its half-destroyed state, the arena still had a high outer wall, broken in places but solid in others. And at the end of the avenue they were currently on was one of the still-high and solid walls. Blinking and twitching her face to pull up the view of the nearest tactical drone, Chu Hua could see that the closest break in the wall big enough to admit a mech was about a hundred meters down a side street. As they neared the end of the avenue, she saw Parkins drift his mech to the right, readying to make the turn toward that gap. She started to drift her mech after his but then stopped when she took another second to analyze the arena wall in front of them.

It only took her a fraction of a moment to make her decision based on what she'd seen. And she knew that what she was about to try would probably go very poorly. But if it didn't...

Parakeet lost some control rounding the corner at a full run but recovered and sprinted his mech toward the distant break in the wall. Chu Hua didn't follow him into the turn. Instead, she concentrated on her rhythm, feeling her arms and legs moving in perfect harmony with her mech until the exact right moment, when her right foot hit the perfect spot she was aiming for...and she launched.

It was a jump, really, nothing special. But 'launch' just seemed the better word as Chu Hua used her forward momentum and the full power of her suit's leg servos to propel the massive machine into the air and directly at the wall in front of her. The wall itself was far too high for her to clear in a single jump, but in her study of its surface, she had noticed something that Parakeet had either missed or ignored.

Exactly 15.4 meters up the side of the wall—her HUD had provided the measurement—was a small concrete ledge that looked as if it might have once been the landing for an external fire escape but was now little more than twisted rebar supporting crumbling cement. But it might just be enough. Of course, the training mech was only rated for jumps as high as 14.6 meters, but hey, Feng was used to breaking the rules of what these machines were supposedly capable of. And she hoped that her increased forward momentum, still more than the mech's max speed, would translate into a higher jump.

She was right, but only barely. As she flew toward the ledge, she brought both of the mech's legs up as high as they would go, bending the hip and knee servos to their stopping points. Even with that, the bottoms of the machine's feet cleared the ledge with only centimeters to spare. As soon as they did, Feng kicked down as fast and as hard as she could.

She felt the mech's feet hit the ledge underneath her and felt the ledge collapse under the impact. But right before it did, she got barely enough purchase to launch her mech vertically just a little bit more. About five meters, maybe even less, and for a moment, she thought she'd miscalculated.

The top of the wall seemed far away, and her upward momentum started to slow as she lost her fight with gravity. Chu Hua braced herself for the long fall back to the street, now almost twenty meters below. That would hurt, even in the mech. But with one last grunt of effort, she reached the suit's bulky right hand as high as its servos would allow. And just as gravity finally won the battle and the mech reached its zenith and started to fall, she felt her mechanical fingers grasp a low point in the uneven upper edge of the bombed-out wall.

She hung there for a second, high above the street below, and quickly sent the command to lock the fingers in place. Then she pulled.

The mech did most of the work, its right arm's augmented strength enough to pull its full ton-and-a-half weight upward toward the wall's upper edge. But even so, Feng felt her muscles stretch and strain under the effort—the training mechs were meant to rely partially on user strength, multiplying it but not entirely replacing it. And she might as well have felt every ounce of the mech's weight on her arm before she was finally able to get the machine's left forearm—the one with the rocket launcher in place of a hand—up and over the wall to help with lifting it. It felt like several seconds to her, but in a much shorter time, she had raised the mech high enough to get her left leg slung over the wall. There, she perched precariously on the less than half-meter uneven edge, staring down into the arena and getting her first glimpse of the primary target—the boss.

It was another mech. But not a training mech like hers; rather, it was a full combat mech, two tons of enough destructive power to level half a small city. And right now, it was turning to face the gap in the wall where Parakeet was about to appear. Whether that meant its driver hadn't seen her or simply didn't think he or she needed to worry about her getting over the wall, Feng didn't know. But it left the enemy mech's back exposed to her for the barest of moments.

Still balancing her mech's belly on the wall, Chu Hua lifted her left arm as quickly as she dared and pointed her twin-barreled rocket launcher squarely at the boss's transparent dome. The instant her HUD signaled missile lock, she twitched her left trigger finger just the right way to empty both barrels and send two dummy missiles streaking straight for the enemy.

It wouldn't be enough, she knew with a sinking in her stomach. A full paramilitary-spec mech like the one she faced could absorb up to six missiles before it would be enough to immobilize or destroy it. And that assumed that none of the mech's countermeasures kicked in to intercept and destroy the missiles mid-flight.

But it was all Feng could do as she felt part of the wall give way beneath her, and her world turned end over end again as the mech plummeted toward the arena floor below.

Chu Hua woke up slowly to a light in her eyes that was far too bright. It sent pain shooting through her head that rivaled even the pain her enacter gene made her feel whenever she even thought about disobeying a direct order. For a moment, she couldn't figure out where she was. Then, she blinked the tears out of her eyes, and the room came into focus, revealing a stark white hospital bay lit by only a dim overhead light that still managed to feel like a sun shining directly in her face.

"You're finally awake," a gruff voice said next to her, and she painfully turned her head to see an older man in a white lab coat staring down at her with a frown.

"What happened?" she asked with an effort, the words hard to push out of her dry throat and lips.

"You had quite the fall in that mech of yours," the man answered, checking some readouts on a screen next to her bed. "Landing head-first, right on your dome. All in all, gave you a pretty bad concussion; would have easily killed you if not for the mech itself."

"What?" she asked, not quite believing what the man—the doctor—was telling her.

"I wasn't there," he said, shrugging, "but I've seen the vid. That was a monumentally stupid thing you did. Has everyone excited for some reason, too."

She was about to ask him to explain that statement, but he walked out of the space, throwing aside the bay's curtain and leaving without a backward glance. But in his place, another face peered around the curtain and lit up in a broad smile.

Jackson Rodriguez was a pugnacious native of Reunion who was only six centimeters taller than Feng but must have weighed twice as much. He was short enough to fit in the cockpit of a mech but almost too wide, and he often complained of horrible chafing in the few times when he and Chu Hua were alone. She just always thought it was funny how his mech always seemed to walk with a swagger all its own, caused by his too-thick legs trying to work the controls meant for someone far skinnier.

"So," he said jovially, "it's true. Your head really is as hard as your mech's."

She tried to smile back and even laugh, but it quickly turned into a wince as the pain in her head surged back. Jackson saw and gave her a wince of his own.

"You look terrible," he said as he moved to the bedside and looked down at her. "But your mech looks worse."

She frowned, but this time, it had nothing to do with the pain. "Did I break it?"

He nodded solemnly. "Just a bit. I mean, blast! What were you thinking going over that wall? The instructors can't even figure out how you did it. They keep saying it was an impossible move. But you did it, so I guess it wasn't. And that really seems to tick them off for some reason."

Feng wasn't sure whether to smile or frown even more at the thought of their instructors scratching their collective heads while watching the video of her unlikely jump over that wall. She settled on a wince as yet another sharp pain coursed through her head.

Was that pain from thinking ill of her instructors—her enacter gene did that sometimes—or was it simply from the head injury?

"Anyway," Jackson continued, "they've got the mechanics taking your mech apart and examining it piece-by-piece to see if you somehow snuck in an illegal mod. I'd tell them they're wasting their time, but they wouldn't listen to a noob like me." He shrugged. "I'm just glad you're safe."

Now, she did smile, if only to reassure him. There wasn't much time for dating or anything like it in the Mechanized Warfare School, but she and Jackson had instantly taken to each other. If there had been more time... Well, no use wondering about what could never be. In the meantime, they'd managed to steal a few quiet moments alone and away from the prying eyes of the instructors.

"Am I in trouble?" she asked him seriously now.

He shrugged again. "Don't know. Half the instructors seem to want to kill you for breaking your mech. But O'Donnell's talking like he wants to give you a medal for that crazy stunt. He keeps telling the others that you're redefining mech warfare, whatever that's supposed to mean. I think he just loves to see them all running around in a tizzy, trying to figure out what to do with you." He smiled wider.

She smiled back again, even though it caused another flash of pain in her head. Master Sergeant Rourke O'Donnell was the oldest of their instructors at the Warfare School and the only one who wasn't an officer. But he commanded the respect of most of the other instructors as one of the GPF's most experienced and decorated mech drivers. The few officers who doubted and even belittled him at first meeting usually changed their tunes pretty quickly when he beat them soundly in one-on-one combat on the practice field. Having him on her side was a very good thing, especially as she tried to explain why she'd broken a multi-million-credit training mech.

"You know he was driving the boss mech, right?" Jackson asked her. He must have seen her look of confusion. "O'Donnell; he was driving that mech in the bombed-out arena. Said he didn't even know you were there; coming in behind Parakeet like that kept you hidden from his sensors until you got on that wall, and then his mech's AI actually flagged and hid your signature as a false contact since you were doing something no training mech should have been capable of. The first he actually knew you were there was when your two dummy missiles hit his dome."

She smiled again. Then she frowned. "Did Parkins...?"

Jackson shook his head. "Nope. O'Donnell took him out before he fired a shot. It was Slider and Hopscotch working together who finally took him down, but only because your two missiles weakened his stats. But even they didn't get him before he'd taken out two-thirds of us." His smile turned sheepish. "Got me with missiles straight to the dome before I even got within a hundred meters."

Chu Hua nodded at this. The big warfare mechs could take a beating. So, technically, could the training mechs. But the instructors programmed them to be 'dead' after only a single missile shot; the better to train the cadets not to get hit in the first place. Even a very lucky shot to the right spot with the right kind of missile or armor-piercing railgun round could take out a full warfare mech, though it was rare.

"So, what happens now?" she asked her friend.

He shrugged. "Now, you recover while I go get chewed out for finishing in the bottom half...again. Then, you can probably stand there while O'Donnell himself chews you out while secretly admiring you for what you did out there. But for now, enjoy the rest. You're gonna need it."

Feng Chu Hua stood ramrod straight, stretching her full 1.4-meter height for the little it was worth, while Master Sergeant Rourke O'Donnell studied her with a hard gaze across his desk in his modest instructor's office.

He let her stand like that for a full minute while he surveyed her, and his frown deepened. Then, he finally waved a hand to motion her to stand at ease.

"Feng," he said gruffly. "You may be the best mech driver I've ever seen come out of this school."

For a second, Chu Hua didn't register the words, delivered as they were in the same tone the man might have used to dress down a cadet for a uniform infraction. When she finally did, she felt her mouth twitch up in a smile but stopped herself. One did not smile at anything Master Sergeant O'Donnell said unless you very quickly wanted a reason to frown instead.

"The problem with you," the man continued, "is that you may also be one of the worst drivers I've seen."

She couldn't help it; she may have suppressed her smile a second ago, but now her mouth dropped open. *How can I be both the best and worst?* she thought. She wanted to ask him but, with great effort, held her tongue.

It didn't matter because he proceeded to tell her anyway. "You see, you can make that mech do amazing things, but you don't play well with others, and you fight every battle with a chip on your shoulder. Makes you completely worthless in unit engagements, and as a result, you'll never rise above private rank if you can't figure out how to be part of a team."

He let that hang in the air, his eyes boring into hers and daring her to argue. She almost did but wisely pulled herself back and continued her silent act.

O'Donnell nodded as if he approved of her restraint. "Your scores are high enough to graduate, just barely. So, I can't stop you from going into the GPF and driving one of those two-ton monstrosities around. Even when what I'd rather do is keep you here for another cycle and force you to break those bad habits of yours." He paused and glared at her as if daring her to argue.

When she still said nothing, he nodded again and continued. "No, I can't hold you back. So, I'll do the next best thing." He raised his watch arm and made a throwing motion toward her with it. Chu Hua felt her own watch, where she clasped her hands behind her, vibrate as it received whatever O'Donnell had sent to it.

"Your unit assignment," he told her. "You're not supposed to get it until after the graduation ceremony tomorrow, but you don't seem the type who cares much about the rules. Makes you a terrible enacter, but maybe a good soldier at the end of the day." She wished he would explain that statement more, but he didn't. "I've pulled some strings and gotten you assigned to the best mech sergeant still on active duty. She'll knock some sense into that thick head of yours."

He regarded her for another moment while she fought very hard to keep her watch behind her and resist the overwhelming urge to pull it up and look at her post-graduation assignment.

"Dismissed!" he barked, and she drew back up to attention, saluting and then beating a hasty retreat. She made it all the way back out into the hall before she checked her watch.

THREE
RUNNING THE COURSE
PRIVATE FENG CHU HUA, GPF

ELEVEN MONTHS AGO – 730 P.D.

"Do it again, Sprite!"

Private Feng Chu Hua winced at the nickname, even though Sergeant Sarah Nowak never said it with the same mocking disdain she'd heard from her fellow cadets back at the Guard Mechanized Warfare School. But she still didn't like it.

Nevertheless, she obeyed the order and started again running through the complicated obstacle course that Nowak had set up for her. The course, nicknamed the 'grinder', was infinitely customizable, and Nowak seemed to have a very creative sadistic streak whenever she altered it for one of Chu Hua's private evening training sessions.

Tonight, the course more than lived up to its name. Chu Hua jogged back to the starting line, going through her last run in her head to try and determine what she could have done better. But as soon as she arrived at the line, the light turned green, and she sprinted forward, shoving aside the analysis and just...feeling.

The first obstacle was simple enough: a ten-meter wall. Feng jumped her mech right over it, landing on the other side and allowing the massive servos in the legs to absorb the impact of all two tons of the combat mech hitting the ground hard. She'd actually seen another private break his legs doing a similar jump just a week ago, as he failed to let his legs go loose at the right moment. That had caused the compression of his mech suit's legs to battle directly against the rigid muscles and bones of his natural legs. Unsurprisingly, the mech won, and the boy's femurs had both snapped, one of them all the way through. He had been screaming when the medics had removed him from the suit.

Chu Hua had no such problems and landed neatly. Then, she was on to the second obstacle. This was a wide pit and required a different kind of jump, aiming for distance, not height. Once again, she executed it perfectly and landed without issue on the other side.

But the third obstacle was harder. It required her to maintain all of her forward momentum from the long jump over the pit and almost immediately use it to leap across yet another pit, but this one too wide to clear in a single leap. Instead, she had to aim for the top of a narrow pillar—wide enough for only one of her suit's massive feet—in the center of the pit and then immediately leap the remaining distance from there.

She landed slightly off-center on the pillar, but not enough to slow her down, and then landed gratefully on the other side of the chasm.

From there, she sprinted down the two-hundred-meter straightaway that led to the fourth obstacle. This one was another wall, but too high for her to jump over. Instead, she had to find the weak spot by using her mech's sensors to measure the thickness along the entire expanse of the wall. Normally, that wouldn't be a problem, but the course was programmed to only allow her suit to find the weakest spot when she was within ten meters of it. At a space-eating sprint of fifteen meters per second, that meant she had only a fraction of an instant to react. And because the weak spot moved every time she ran the course, she couldn't use her prior experience to help her guess where it would be.

Most mech drivers in the GPF would slow their mechs down right before the wall, figuring it was better to lose a second or two in doing so instead of losing a lot more time and a damage penalty from hitting the wall in the wrong place. But Feng didn't like to do it that way. In typical fashion for her, she charged headlong and full out at the wall, timing herself to when she would hit the ten-meter mark.

When she did, she barely had time to register the red outline of the weak spot, seven meters up and three to her left. She planted her right foot hard and pushed off, juking her mech to the left, and then immediately planted and pushed off with her left foot, propelling the massive machine through the air.

She hit the weak spot almost dead center, and the wall crumbled around her. Then she fell. Only the fall was much more than the seven meters she'd had to jump up to hit the weak spot because on the other side of the wall was another deep and wide chasm. Hanging above that chasm, slightly off-center, was the boom of a large crane. Chu Hua lifted her left arm and twitched her trigger finger—she had already selected the right ammunition before hitting the wall—and a small rocket left her launcher, trailing a thin but incredibly strong cable. As the rocket neared the crane's boom, it broke apart, revealing a grappling claw, and grabbed one of the boom's struts. With a jerk that jarred her arm even inside the suit, her downward fall arrested, and she began to swing at the end of the cable in a pendulum arc that ended with her landing almost gently on the chasm's opposite edge.

Chu Hua checked her time, pleased to see that she was a full two seconds ahead of her previous course best. But now she was nearing the most difficult and time-eating obstacle, and the one that truly illustrated Sarah Nowak's sadistic side.

Ahead of her were six more cranes, three to either side of the designated path, but each of these had wrecking balls swinging from them that moved in somehow beautifully overlapping but carefully choreographed arcs that never allowed them to hit each other, but also left very little space for Chu Hua to navigate through.

Of course, it still wasn't that easy. Feng switched her HUD view to infrared and saw the other terrible part of this obstacle. Along the path through which the wrecking balls traversed, seemingly at random heights and angles, she could now see the straight and glowing paths of more than a dozen lasers. She had less than a second to study their positions before she hit the outer edge of the obstacle path.

She threw her mech into a roll as one of the wrecking balls swung down at dome level. Then, coming out of the roll, she immediately leapt into the air, twisting the mech to the left as she did so to avoid two laser beams: one at knee level and the other vertically intersecting it at an angle. She landed on the other side and then ducked as another wrecking ball swung by overhead. Coming up from her crouch, she propelled her mech up and forward in a diving leap, barely clearing another two lasers that formed two sides of an upside-down triangle with its zenith at waist level.

On she went, dancing her mech around swinging balls of destruction and going up, over, and around wildly crisscrossing beams of infrared light. She could see the end of the obstacle path now and had only two more wrecking balls to clear, plus another half dozen lasers. She juked quickly to the right, planting her foot and pushing off. But instead of jumping, she let her mech fall to the left, hitting the ground on her side and then rolling forward, barely going under a pair of beams overhead and missing the second-to-last wrecking ball that came straight at her down the middle of the path.

Almost there. She got back to her feet just in time to jump over a low beam and then crouch and roll to her left to avoid the final wrecking ball, then immediately roll to her right to avoid another vertical laser beam. She was so close now to the end, and she stood again and then launched herself vertically toward a small gap between two lasers that sat parallel to the ground, one low and one high, but close enough together that she had to bring her mech's knees to its chest to fit through the gap between them.

The 'safe' line for this particular obstacle was now just a meter away, and there was nothing between her and it. But just before she stepped over it, something slammed into her back and sent her tumbling forward, her suit kicking up a massive cloud of dust as it hit the dirt just over the line and rolled through it.

Blast, she thought as she quickly regained control. *That second-to-last wrecking ball caught me on the backswing.* She'd thought she was moving fast enough to avoid it but apparently had miscalculated. Still, there was nothing to do about it other than continue onward. She ran around the pillar that marked the turnaround point for the course, then easily tackled the three remaining obstacles on the backstretch, none as hard as the fourth one, but enough to cause her to pant with exhaustion when she finally crossed the finish line.

Only at that point did she allow herself to check her time again. And with an exultant cry, she saw she'd still beaten her best mark, even with the five-second damage penalty from the wrecking ball that hit her.

She turned her dome toward Sarah Nowak, who was sitting calmly and nonchalantly in a folding chair by the course's finish line. Her face was expressionless, but Chu Hua still hoped she would get some word of praise from her sergeant for besting all her previous times on this particular course, which she'd already run three other times this evening.

But, to Feng's chagrin, Nowak only shook her head slowly. "You got hit," she said simply.

"Yes, ma'am," Chu Hua replied, "but I still bested my time."

Nowak frowned. "But in a combat situation, you'd have much more than a time penalty. You'd possibly be dead. You'll need to run it again, perfectly this time."

Chu Hua's heart sank. It was already eight in the evening, and she was exhausted. Despite the combat mechs requiring very little muscle strength to operate, they still required the wearer to make all of the moves with their bodies that they wanted the mech suits to make. Even with strength augmentation, that was enough to wipe out any driver after even a few minutes of operating at full speed. And after four times through the course, Chu Hua felt she couldn't even walk another step in her suit, much less run, jump, and swing like she just had.

She searched Sarah Nowak's face for any hint of sympathy or sign that she was joking. But the sergeant maintained the same bored expression she almost always did, giving away nothing, her hand resting on her swollen, pregnant belly as she waited for Chu Hua to follow her order. Sighing, Feng turned her mech and moved slowly—buying herself as much time to rest as possible—back to the starting line.

FOUR
PLAYING IN THE PARK
PRIVATE FENG CHU HUA, GPF

FIVE MONTHS AGO – 731 P.D.

The sound of children laughing and screaming as they scurried over a nearby play structure was so unusual for Feng Chu Hua that she felt like she'd entered a parallel dimension of some sort. But it was only the small park a few blocks from the Guard Paramilitary Force Base on Greater York, where Feng had agreed to meet her friend and mentor, Sergeant Sarah Nowak, and her family for a Sunday afternoon chat.

Sarah herself was cooing and playing with Geneva, her two-month-old baby, who was gurgling happily in the stroller next to the picnic table. Feng was watching her in disbelief. Nowak was a hard-charging, strict disciplinarian when it came to the mech drivers in her squad. For months, Chu Hua had thought that Sarah hated her and was trying to drum her out of the GPF, giving her all sorts of extra drills at the end of every day when the rest of the squad had already hit the showers and the chow line.

It had turned out, thankfully, that Sarah had seen Chu Hua's potential and was actually giving her extra training to make sure she could meet her full capabilities driving one of the massive mechs. But she'd been so stingy with the compliments that Feng had thought the older woman was going to dismiss her from the unit at the end of each and every day. Until one day, out of the blue, when Feng had been minutes away from quitting, Sarah had invited her to dinner with her family off-base. There, she had met Octavio Nowak, Sarah's husband, for the first time and heard the first words of praise she'd ever received from Sarah's mouth.

Now, watching that same woman with her infant daughter, playing peek-a-boo, was so incongruous with the normally taciturn and strict woman from her training that Chu Hua really felt reality was on a bender.

"She ignoring you and playing with the baby again?" a cheerful masculine voice broke Chu Hua's thoughts, and she looked up and smiled at Octavio Nowak. He sat down across the table from the two women and slid one of the two beer bottles he was holding across to Feng.

"One for you," he said, "and one for me. And none for the nursing mother."

Sarah threw her husband the same look she gave to new recruits who got rowdy in their mechs. It could normally cause even hardened guardsmen to shrink and apologize profusely, but Octavio, 'Tavi' to his wife and friends, took it in stride with a smirk directed back at his red-haired wife.

"You shouldn't tease her like that," Feng said lightly. "She'll take it out on me when she gets back. She'll make me walk across the bottom of Lake Gaul in my mech again and count the fish."

Tavi laughed so hard he spit out the sip of beer he'd taken, setting down the bottle and wiping the liquid out of his beard with both hands. "She did not make you do that! Wait, did she?"

Sarah turned and regarded the most junior private in her squad with an evil grin. "Of course I did. And I'll make her do it again, *without* the mech, just for that comment."

Now, it was Feng's turn to laugh. Luckily, she hadn't started drinking her beer yet, so she didn't have the same cleanup job that Tavi had.

The man regarded the two women with a smirk as he took a new sip of his drink. "You mech drivers are all crazy."

"Hey," Sarah protested. "You married one. You know you like the thought of me in that big machine making all those regs run for cover. It's why you were attracted to me in the first place."

Tavi raised his eyebrows and regarded his wife with a playful grin. "Actually, it was your butt that attracted me to you," he said deadpan. "But the whole mech thing was enough to convince me I could never break up with you, or you'd come after me."

Sarah picked up a toy from Geneva's stroller and threw it at her husband's head. He didn't dodge but let the stuffed elephant bounce off his forehead before changing his expression to one of exaggerated hurt. "Oh yeah," his wife chided. "Well, the joke's on you. Having this little one made my butt huge. So now you don't even have that!"

Tavi grinned again and winked at Feng. "I like her big butt even more," he mock whispered.

Chu Hua laughed again as Sarah's eyes went wide, and her mouth fell open at her husband's irreverent comment. "You'll pay for that later, Octavio Antoni Nowak," she said in feigned anger.

"Promise?" the man replied with another wink, this time directed at his wife.

"You guys!" gasped Chu Hua. "I'm never going to be able to drink my beer if you keep this up! Watching you two is just so...gross."

All three of them laughed heartily, with Sarah pinching the baby Geneva's little feet to keep the girl placated while the adults fought tears of mirth from their eyes.

The banter continued for another few minutes until Geneva got fussy, and Sarah got up to walk the stroller around a path that encircled the park.

Alone at the table, Feng and Tavi sipped their beers and watched the children play on the nearby structure.

"I wish I had this," Feng said softly as she watched a little boy go down a slide and fly off the end, landing on his butt in the sand and laughing hysterically at himself.

"What?" Tavi asked, raising an eyebrow. "You want a bunch of kids?"

"No," she said. "Well, maybe someday. No, I just wish I had what you and Sarah have. It never seemed possible, you know?"

"Why, because you're an enacter?" The question was a serious one, but his tone remained playful enough to take the sting out of it.

She shrugged. "Yeah. There aren't exactly men lining up to marry enacter women. And all of the enacter men my age are so wrapped up in getting ahead and promoted that they aren't looking for anything serious. And I refuse to be anyone's one-night stand." She meant the words to come out as playfully as Tavi's question, but even she recognized the genuine frustration in her tone.

"Chu Hua, I pity any man that thinks he can take advantage of you," Octavio said lightly, returning a measure of levity to the mood. But then he looked at her with a serious expression. "Look, I know Sarah and I make it look easy sometimes. But it takes more work than either of us care to admit. She's loyal to the Council first, and I know that; she has no choice. I had to make my peace with it early on, but that doesn't make it easy or uplifting to know that my wife's first commitment isn't to me. And it sure isn't easy for her to know that there's such a massive part of her life that I can never be a part of or even understand, you know?"

Feng looked at him with sympathy. "Is it really that hard?"

He nodded, a solemn smile on his lips. "It is. So hard. For both of us. But also so worth it. I wouldn't have it any other way. Because even though I know my wife can't make a lot of her own decisions, I at least know she chose me. And that feels pretty good when she isn't threatening to stomp on me with her mech, that is." His smile widened.

She smiled back. "You're one of a kind, Tavi. You have any brothers I don't know about?"

He shrugged. "Only a sister, and I wouldn't wish her on my worst enemy. If anyone should have been born an enacter, it's Zofia. Would have saved the galaxy a whole lot of hurt, that's for sure."

They both laughed lightly and took another sip of their respective drinks.

"But seriously," Tavi continued. "You'll find what you're looking for. If it happens like it did for me and Sarah, it will take you by surprise, and before you know it, you'll be married with a kid on the way. Assuming that's what you want."

She shrugged. "I don't know. Maybe I'll start by just wishing for a man who isn't trying to kill me in his mech to impress the officers. Work my way from there. Not sure about the kids, though. Sometimes, I find myself wishing I had a baby just like Geneva. Other times, I can't imagine having to care for another human being like that."

"Well, Geneva isn't sleeping through the night right now, so we may be willing to rent her out to you in the evenings for a modest fee."

The somber mood broke, and Feng laughed and enjoyed the feel of the sun on her skin as she and Octavio talked of inconsequential things until Sarah returned and the afternoon's outing ended all too soon.

FIVE
DEPLOYMENT ORDERS
PRIVATE FENG CHU HUA, GPF

FOUR WEEKS AGO – 731 P.D.

"Council observers report that the rebels are killing civilians in a vain effort to show the Panamar planetary prefecture just how serious they are. It's bad here on the ground, with shots fired every few minutes and the screams of the dying filling the air in between. Only one thing is certain: the Guard must respond and bring order back to this planet before more innocents die."

Sarah turned the vidscreen off, cutting short the report from Galactic News Service, and peered with a frown at her squad. Chu Hua could feel the older woman's stress radiating off her like heat from an oven, but Nowak's face was calm other than a tight-lipped frown.

"Word from above is, we go," Sarah said, drawing nods from the other three GPF soldiers in the room.

"When, Sarge?" Corporal Harrison Walker asked.

"Three days. Get your affairs in order and say goodbye to your loved ones."

"Aw, Sarge, ain't no one love Walker. He's good to go now!" joked Private Samuel Jennings, the youngest squad member aside from Chu

Hua. Walker threw the boy a side-eyed frown, but there was mirth in his eyes.

"Well, then you'll need all three days to say goodbye to your action figures," Walker quipped back.

"Alright, alright, can it!" Sarah said, though there was no anger in her tone, just worry. "Be here at 0700 sharp on Tuesday for a prelaunch briefing. Until then, dismissed!"

Walker and Jennings immediately bolted for the door while Sarah walked over to sit at the small desk she shared with the four other sergeants in Lieutenant Jose Sandoval's 17th Platoon. Chu Hua hung back, unsure of how to ask what she wanted. She was searching for the right words when Nowak looked up as if just noticing her youngest squad member was still there.

"Something on your mind, Private Feng?"

Chu Hua swallowed. "Uh, Sarge, it's just that...well, it's my first deployment. I'm a little..."

"Nervous? Scared? Freaked out?" Sarah guessed. At Chu Hua's timid nod, she continued. "Listen, we've all been there. I still remember my first deployment, on Phoenix actually, just one system over from Panamar. Bunch of settlers there decided that they wanted to self-govern. They sent my platoon in, and we made short work of it. But I remember the first time a real bullet hit my mech's dome. Scared me so bad I didn't sleep that night—couldn't stop shaking."

"So, what did you do about it?" Chu Hua asked.

Sarah shrugged. "Nothing to do but just keep going. I got up the next day and kept fighting. By the time a dozen more bullets had hit my dome without so much as scratching it, I stopped jumping every time one came close." She paused, regarding Chu Hua with a half-smile. "Look, we can tell you over and over again in training just how close to invincible we are in our suits, but deep down, you're just not going to believe it until you take some solid hits and see for yourself. You'll be fine. Just remember your training and rely on your squad mates, and we'll all come out of this OK, especially given the light arms Guard Intel reports the Panamarian rebels are using."

"Yes, Sarge. Uh, thank you, Sarge." Chu Hua turned to go, but Sarah's voice caught her before she left the squad briefing room.

"Feng? Why don't you come over for dinner tonight? We can talk more if you need it."

Chu Hua turned back with a grateful smile. "I appreciate that, Sarge, but I don't want to intrude on your family time before a deployment."

Sarah laughed lightly. "Actually, given how I expect Octavio to react to the news, you'll be doing me a favor. I could use a buffer at dinner. Be there at 18:30 sharp. Got it?"

"See you there, Sarge. And...thanks."

Nowak nodded and returned to her paperwork. Chu Hua left the room, her step a little lighter than before.

SIX
REVELATIONS
PRIVATE FENG CHU HUA, GPF

PRESENT DAY

"Walker, Feng, get up here!" the voice of Sergeant Sarah Nowak echoed in the dome of Feng Chu Hua's massive two-ton mech.

"Coming, Sarge!" Chu Hua responded, twitching her nose and pursing her lips to instruct her heads-up display to pinpoint her squad leader's location. It showed Nowak's flashing green dot two streets over and a block forward of her current position.

Feng immediately started moving her mech in that direction, using the same space-eating rhythm that she'd grown accustomed to in her training mech over a year ago. In less than a minute, she reached Sergeant Nowak's location just before Corporal Harrison Walker tromped up in his own mech. "How'd you beat me here, Sprite?" Walker asked her playfully through a private comm channel so Nowak wouldn't hear. "You speeding again?"

Chu Hua laughed. "Traffic was light, Corporal."

Talk ceased as Nowak highlighted the situation in their HUDs. They were on the south side of San Sebastian, Panamar's capital city.

Across the road from them, three rebel troops were holed up in a streetside cafe, their red outlines hunkered down underneath the building's wide windows. Feng was about to ask for instructions when an alarm went off in the confines of her suit, and she heard Sarah's voice on the comm, yelling, "Anti-matter detected! Take 'em. Now!"

Following the program Nowak transmitted to her and Walker, Feng raised the left arm of her suit and launched a rocket straight at the enemy outline furthest to the right, while Nowak took the one in the middle and Walker the one on the left. All three projectiles simultaneously bored into the concrete wall of the café, directly in front of each of the three hidden hostiles. In a fraction of a second, they'd burrowed in far enough, and then, in near-perfect unison, each projectile's little brain detonated the shaped charge in its nose.

Chu Hua was grateful she couldn't actually see the three rebels as each rocket's shaped charge pulverized the cafe wall and turned it into a shotgun blast of gravel and shrapnel. She'd seen the aftermath of a blast like that for the first time just a few days before, several kilometers south of their current location. In that case, there hadn't been enough of the rebel soldier left to identify the body's gender. It had been disgusting but also somewhat awe-inspiring. After all, they didn't give that kind of firepower to just anyone.

Immediately following the blast, Nowak leapt her mech forward and crashed through what remained of the cafe wall and windows. Feng and Walker followed closely to either side. Inside, they found an abattoir of blood and body parts, plus a very scary-looking weapon covered in the blood and brain matter of its former owner.

"Blast, Sarge! An AM launcher?" Walker said in an excited tone. "How did the rebs get their hands on Guard tech?"

"I heard it's like this all over the city," Feng chimed in. "These are more than just rebels with home-printed ARs. I mean, an anti-matter launcher in the middle of the slums of Panamar? The tech level here isn't close to enough to make that. That didn't come from any Edge planet." She thought that observation was a fairly astute one.

"Can the chatter, 2nd Squad!" intruded the voice of Lieutenant Sandoval on all of their comms. "Nowak, Feng, survey the site for further intel and report anything you find to the command post.

Walker! You bring that AP launcher back to the CP now. Nowak and Feng can finish up there."

"Roger that!" Walker and Feng chorused while Nowak responded, "Sir!". And with that, Feng didn't even get to hear how Sarah might have responded to her comments on the AM Launcher's origin. As enacters, none of them could disobey the lieutenant's orders. And he'd told them to 'can the chatter', though that was sufficiently vague that they could probably talk about it later when they were done following the man's immediate orders.

Chu Hua did as she was told and began to systematically search the cafe, her mech hunched over in a way that hurt her back, as the cafe ceiling wasn't high enough to fit the three-meter-tall behemoth. She was making her first sweep across the restaurant floor when she saw the table with some strange-looking things on top of it. Was that paper?

"Sarge, you may want to look at this," she called over to Sarah, who finished watching Walker gingerly carry the AM launcher out of the café and then worked her way over to Chu Hua's side.

Sarah joined Feng where she was already looking at the pamphlets on the table in front of her. She recognized them as the same they'd seen in other parts of the city: printed copies of the so-called 'Revelations', the bunch of lies about the Council and some enacter who had supposedly disobeyed their orders. Nothing but malarkey in her opinion; there was no way any enacter could ever disobey the Council...

"Second Squad, no one can see those lying pamphlets." Sandoval's words broke her musings; she'd been obediently streaming video of the find back to the CP for him to see. "Torch the whole place and then continue your sweep of that sector."

Chu Hua immediately turned and ignited the flamethrower housed alongside her left arm's launcher and began dutifully incinerating her side of the café. As she did so, she caught a glance of Sarah's mech, still hunched over the offending pamphlets. She couldn't see the older woman's face through the glare on her dome, but the stance of the big machine seemed to impart a tense feeling. And why was she hesitating? Was she...*reading* the pamphlets?

"Sarge, you OK?" she asked through the suit comms.

The other mech seemed to shake itself, and Sarah ignited her own flamethrower, incinerating the pamphlets on the table in front of her.

"Sure, Feng. I'm fine. Just a cramp."

But Chu Hua wasn't so sure.

Sarah hadn't come to the mess hall with the rest of them. That only increased Feng's worry for her. Because she was increasingly convinced that it hadn't been her imagination; Sarah really had hesitated before burning those pamphlets. That had to have been painful for the woman. The enacter gene was a vicious mutation sometimes. Even the barest hesitation in following a direct order could cause an enacter so much pain that he or she would be little better than a puddle on the ground.

The pain always started in the head, and for most enacters, that's where it stayed. Chu Hua had once heard it aptly described as the feeling of someone sticking a knife in each of your temples and then moving them around to scramble your brains while you were awake and aware of it every second. It was agonizing.

So, if Sarah had deliberately put herself through even a fraction of that pain, she had to have had a good reason. Only Feng couldn't figure out what it might be. They all knew what those blasted 'Revelations' from the pamphlets said. Just over three months ago, someone had hacked the Net, and a video of Kendra Siefred, a respected senior assembly member, and Todd Crowley, a well-known journalist, had played on all streams. In the recording, Siefred and Crowley had spouted all sorts of lies about the Council, essentially calling it nothing more than a despotic government ruled by the Keeper, the head of the Assembly.

Furthermore, they'd made the ridiculous and outlandish claim that the government had been trying to poison the people with something in their food and water that would turn ordinary people into enacters. It was preposterous in the extreme, and Feng had found herself easily distrusting the words. But there was one part she *hadn't* been able to get past entirely: the story of Tyrus Tyne.

Tyne had supposedly been an alpha, one of the near-mythical secret police that reported directly to the Council and did their bidding. The revelation of the Alpha program's existence in Siefred's and Crowley's recording hadn't been all that surprising to Chu Hua, but what *had* been was the claim that Tyne, an enacter himself, had somehow disobeyed the Council and rebelled against them. Not only was that patently impossible, but if true, it would be concerning beyond measure. After all, if enacters could choose for themselves, it would be chaos. Sure, many of them, like Chu Hua, would continue to obey the Council, recognizing its vital place in keeping the peace. But others... she'd met a few who might take their newfound freedom and do less-than-savory things with it.

What if that part about Tyne was true? And what would that mean for Feng Chu Hua and the millions of other enacters in the galaxy?

Still, Feng had largely managed to thrust those worries aside. Given that the rest of the Revelations were surely lies, and given the complete impossibility that an enacter like Tyne might have broken his genetic programming, she found it was relatively easy to discount the possibility. She'd thought Sarah would receive them the same way. But if her sergeant, friend, and mentor had gone through that much pain just to look at a bunch of pamphlets...maybe Feng didn't know her as well as she thought she did.

Either way, Nowak not being at dinner was a cause for concern. Sure, she'd made some excuse about staying behind to debrief herself on the squad's performance that day. Corporal Walker and Private Jennings hadn't found anything unusual about that and had shrugged it off and almost ran to the mess hall. Walking around all day in a two-ton mech, even though the machine did most of the work for you, had a tendency to make one really hungry. The mechs fed their drivers water and a protein mixture through a tube whenever they needed it, but it wasn't exactly appetizing. And the menu for tonight was reconstituted mac n' cheese, one of Walker's favorites. Jennings tended to like whatever Walker liked, like a little puppy that followed the man around.

Of course, people said the same thing about Chu Hua and her relationship with Sarah. Nowak was a professional and didn't play favorites in the field or even in training. But everyone knew she had a soft spot for Feng and that Chu Hua looked up to her as more than just her sergeant.

Which was why Chu Hua finished her portion of mac n' cheese and freeze-dried green beans quickly and then made her way back to the temporary barracks that housed 2nd Squad. There, she found her friend still sitting on her cot, reading something Feng couldn't see in her watch's holo field.

"You OK, Sarge?" she asked, trying to sound casual.

Sarah looked up as if she hadn't noticed Chu Hua come in. "Oh, I'm fine, Private. Just reading some mail from home."

Feng smiled. "How are Tavi and Geneva?" The question was a copout. She knew what she wanted to ask Sarah but not how to do it.

Sarah smiled in return, but it didn't reach her eyes. "They're great. Geneva started crawling."

"Oh, that's great! How wonderful..." Chu Hua trailed off when she saw the look on her friend's face. "Oh, Sarge. I'm so sorry you missed that. It must be..." She couldn't find the words; she had no idea what Sarah was actually going through, having no children of her own, but she wanted so badly to be able to sympathize with her.

Nowak must have seen her conflict and smiled again at her. "It's OK, Chu Hua. I'm right where I'm supposed to be. And the sooner we take care of these rebels, the faster I can get home to my little girl. She'll still be there when I get back. And Tavi's sending me vids on every courier ship."

"Can I see?"

Sarah's smile widened. "Sure." She pecked at her holo for a second and dropped the privacy field so that Feng could see a vid of nearly-seven-month-old Geneva levering herself up onto her hands and knees and tentatively pushing herself forward across the rug in the Nowak's small apartment on Greater York. In the background, they could hear Tavi's voice encouraging the little girl. 'Do it for Mama, Geneva. Mama wants to see you crawl.'

The two women laughed as the little girl grinned widely and started moving faster, and then got ahead of herself and face planted into the thick rug. Geneva levered herself back up, looking with wide eyes at the camera with Tavi behind it, before deciding she wasn't hurt and starting to move forward cheerfully again.

They watched a few more vids like that, and Feng let herself conveniently forget why she'd come to talk to Sarah in the first place.

SEVEN
DEATH VALLEY
PRIVATE FENG CHU HUA, GPF

"Second Squad, listen up!" They were gathered in their barracks, each of them standing at attention in front of their respective bunk, when Sarah Nowak entered the room and started briefing them on the day's mission. She had just returned from the larger briefing with the lieutenant and was passing along to them the parts they needed to know about. It was a familiar routine by now and even a comforting one for Chu Hua.

"We're back in the southern sector today; no surprise there. We'll be moving down four parallel avenues in the center of Death Valley." Walker and Jennings both groaned. Death Valley was the name the mech drivers had given to a part of San Sebastian where almost all the fighting had been taking place.

Death Valley was where the city encompassed two hilly areas that rose on either side of a long and narrow depression filled with apartment buildings and commercial areas. The hills themselves were covered in houses, with the eastern hill hosting mostly smaller homes with tiny yards and the western hill hosting some of the city's largest homes, with sprawling estate-like compounds. The depression in between the two hills was called Death Valley because it had seen some of the fiercest fighting in the first days of the battle for San Sebastian, and the regs had taken a few dozen casualties before they'd been withdrawn.

But for the last several days, the mechs had been going into the area. And if the rebels had thought they'd won by taking out a few softies, they'd been far less lucky with the mechanized division. So far, they'd done little to even slow down the massive machines as they'd begun systematically clearing the urban valley of rebel threats.

"We're on point for this one," Sarah continued. "One mech per avenue; we're not anticipating any heavy weapons, but we will have close support from 1st and 3rd Squads behind us and 4th and 5th riding the dropships."

"They're putting us alone in Death Valley? Even with the support Sarge, that sounds risky," Corporal Walker said, wincing visibly as the mere act of even questioning the orders triggered his enacter pain response. But he was only saying out loud what the rest of them were thinking, especially given the AM launcher they'd found the day before.

"Relax, Walker," Sarah chided. "Latest intel says the rebels have largely cleared that part of the city; they're consolidating their forces north of there. This should just be a mop-up exercise with minimal resistance. Hoorah?"

"Hoorah, Sarge," Walker said, and they could see the pain on his face fade.

"OK, grunts," Sarah said. "Mechs are prepped and ready. You have fifteen minutes to be in the dropship. Let's move!"

Twenty-five minutes later, Feng tromped her mech off the dropship and into the streets of San Sebastian and Death Valley. As the dropships had descended, she'd watched civilians scurry for cover, rushing into their apartment buildings or nearby stores to avoid the incoming mechs. The first few times Feng had seen that happen, it had given her an odd sense of melancholy. Didn't these people understand the Guard was here to help them? That the rebels, not the Guard, were the bad guys destroying their city? Now, after two weeks on the ground, it actually made her happy. Fewer civilians in the streets made it easier to find and engage the rebels.

Feng moved her mech out without waiting for further orders. Sarah had already assigned each of them an avenue to move down and clear. Feng's was the middle right, while Sarah's was the middle left. Walker and Jennings took the edges. They were to move down at a fairly steady pace, line abreast although out-of-sight of each other except at intersections. That way, they could move to support each other if any of them hit heavy resistance but still cover maximum ground.

As they moved, loudspeakers mounted on the shoulders of their mechs rotated a series of brief messages in multiple languages, including the local patois mix of Italian and Portuguese, instructing the citizenry to stay inside their homes and to comm the Guard immediately if they knew the locations of any terrorists. To Feng's knowledge, no civilian had once commed the Guard to report on the rebels; it was one more thing that confused her about this place. Wouldn't you want to bring the Guard in to get rid of the selfish men and women who were using your city as a place to violently air their grievances against the only government in the history of humanity that had kept the peace for uninterrupted centuries?

Apparently, Panamar really was a planet of malcontents like the media made it out to be back in the Core worlds. This was Feng's first trip to the Edge, and so far, it had been an eye-opening experience. Greater York and her own homeworld of Huoshan were both heavily urban, with several billion people living on each. The streets were clean, and the buildings sparkled in the warm light of yellow suns. The people were well-dressed, the parks well-kept, and the hovercars shiny and new.

But here on Panamar, the city streets were dirty, both with garbage and with the dust and dirt that somehow came into the city from the surrounding jungles. San Sebastian was quite literally surrounded by jungle, with only a single cracked highway leading out of the city toward Jamestown, the next city that sat a few hundred kilometers to the north. In San Sebastian, the people wore faded clothing that looked like what people in the Core might have worn twenty years ago. The cars, likewise, were older models that appeared to be held together with duct tape more than anything else.

And the sun! The little red star that shone down on Panamar had actually been the biggest problem for the Guard Paramilitary Forces since they'd arrived. Not only was the crimson light so abnormal that it actually caused vertigo for some of the Guard, but they'd had to down Vitamin D supplements and mood enhancers at every meal because the dim star's light had quickly driven some guardmembers into a deep depression.

Of course, the cursed planet was also so close to that little star that the heat was oppressive. Usually, getting out of your mech at the end of a hard day was a relief—the opportunity to stretch weary limbs and joints was an ecstasy they all looked forward to. But not on Panamar. Here, getting out of your climate-controlled mech at the end of the day was like stepping into a sauna, but not in a good way. The air was hot and wet, and Feng usually found herself drenched in sweat within minutes of exiting her mech each evening.

"Second Squad," the voice of Lieutenant Sandoval intruded on Feng's thoughts an hour into their patrol. "Sergeant Nowak is engaging three hostiles at her position. Stand by for possible support."

"Yes, sir," Feng responded, hearing similar acknowledgments from Walker and Jennings. Jennings' voice sounded strained. He had stayed behind at the barracks the previous day fighting a stomach bug that the regs jokingly called Panamar's Revenge. It usually only lasted a day, but Jennings had looked sick even as he'd been getting into his mech this morning. The big machines had plumbing for that sort of thing, but it wasn't really designed for someone having those kinds of issues, and Feng shuddered to think of what the other private was going through already today.

EIGHT
SACRIFICE
SERGEANT SARAH NOWAK, GPF

Sarah stopped her forward progress in the middle of the street and turned to face where the map showed the enemy. There, she saw two men and one woman standing behind a parked hovercar, with their guns pointed in her direction in what they surely thought was a well-planned ambush. They hadn't fired yet; perhaps the speed of the mech's approach had surprised them.

Sarah twitched her nose just so, and the suit picked up on her intent. "Halt!" said a loud, prerecorded male voice from the suit's speakers. "This is the Guard. Lay down your weapons. You are under arrest. Deadly force is authorized."

For a brief second, as Sarah watched the faces of the three rebels magnified in her HUD, she thought and hoped they might actually surrender. But then the woman's face hardened, and Sarah saw her pull the trigger of her assault rifle.

The impacts of multiple railgun rounds hit Sarah in the suit's chest hard enough that the mech shook around her.

"Warning," came another disembodied voice—female this time—in her ear. "Armor-piercing rounds detected. Suit integrity at low-to-moderate risk." An image popped up in the corner of her HUD, an outline of the suit with multiple yellow circles flashing on the chest region where the bullets had hit. *Well, this is unexpected,* she thought grimly.

Sarah brought up her left arm and twitched her pinky finger and then her index finger. A small grenade shot out from the suit's embedded launcher and arced toward the hovercar shielding the three assailants. The rebels saw it coming and tried to react. Two of them, including the woman, ducked back behind the hovercar. The other man dove away from the car toward the doorway of a nearby building.

The grenade hit the car and exploded on impact. A high-explosive round, it was designed to create a pressure wave, not spread shrapnel like a standard anti-personnel grenade. In this case, the shockwave was enough to flip the car over, crushing the two rebels who had tried to hide behind it.

Sarah walked the suit calmly toward the overturned car. Two of the blips on her map now showed flashing red, indicating their vitals were well on their way to ceasing. The third blip, the man who had leapt away from the car, showed flashing yellow. That meant he was injured but still likely combat-effective.

"Halt!" came the loud male voice again from the mech's external speakers. "This is the Guard. Lay down your weapons. You are under arrest."

Sarah saw through the HUD's magnification that the man—now that she was closer, she could see he was more a boy, just a teenager—was stirring, though his gun was several meters from his body. She saw him slowly get up, his hands raised as he shook his head groggily, the pain clear on his face; no doubt the explosion had burst his eardrums. This close to him, she could also see that his clothes hung loose on his overly slim body in a sure sign of malnutrition. She relaxed marginally; this boy was no threat to her mech.

But as he rose, the suit flagged a metallic reading on the hip away from Sarah: likely a pistol in a holster. She readied to fire the assault rifle in her suit's right arm, just in case the boy decided to draw down on her, though a small arm like that would be completely ineffective against her mech.

Instead of drawing his weapon, the boy bolted the remaining two meters toward the doorway he'd been trying to reach, bursting into the apartment building and out of Sarah's direct line of sight.

She would have shaken her head in frustration, but the suit would have interpreted that as a command. So, she just grunted instead.

"Lieutenant," she said, and the mech automatically opened a comm channel to Sandoval. "Two targets down, but a third escaped into an apartment building. Request a squad of regs to clear it."

There was a brief silence on the line as Sandoval considered the ask. While she waited, Sarah studied the building in front of her. It was built from simple concrete blocks fused together, like so much of the drab architecture in Panamar. But unlike the towering buildings around it, it was only five stories and probably didn't even have a lift, just stairs to reach the highest levels. Cheap all around, just like the depressing planet it was built on.

"Negative, Nowak," came Sandoval's voice. "All regulars engaged on the hill east of your position. Can you do a surgical strike?"

Sarah blinked her right eye twice and then her left eye once. The transparent dome around her head darkened, and her HUD switched to thermal imaging, allowing her to see through the building's thin walls and showing her the yellow, orange, and red shapes of the people inside. One of those shapes, now on the second floor, was outlined in a flashing dotted yellow line as the mech's onboard AI made its best guess as to the identity of the injured rebel boy based on his thermal signature. Unfortunately, his image was close to several others, no doubt residents of the apartment he'd chosen to hide in.

Some numbers popped up next to the boy's outline, dominated by a percentage at the top.

"LT, my suit estimates only a sixteen percent chance of successful surgical strike through the building walls. Eighty-four percent chance of civilian collateral. Strongly recommend tagging for the regs once they're available." She said the words in a calm, dispassionate voice, but she could feel a surge of something akin to panic inside her and threatening to creep into her tone. She quickly quashed it down.

"Negative again, Nowak." The lieutenant's words hit her like a death sentence delivered by a judge, and Sarah choked down a gasp of surprise, hoping Sandoval hadn't heard it.

He's just a boy, and the others with him might even be his family, she thought.

"Standing orders are to assume any civilians in the vicinity are harboring the fugitives and are with the rebels," Sandoval continued. "You are ordered to engage with HE penetrators."

"Yes, sir," Sarah answered reluctantly, after only a small outward hesitation. But her mind instantly flashed back to a conversation with her husband, Octavio, on their last night together at home. His voice echoed in her head: 'Have they ever ordered you to do something you knew was wrong?' He'd asked the question in a well-meaning way, but it had been bothering her ever since because she couldn't answer it the way she wanted to, not really.

Or maybe it was more that being a mother made her rethink taking a life.

The pain hit her then. Even her merest hesitation was being interpreted as disobedience by the subconscious part of her brain activated by her enacter gene. It sent a surge of agony through her head that grew by the millisecond as she continued to delay her obedience to the order.

Slowly, Sarah raised her left arm to point it toward the target heat signature, and the pain abated. She twitched her pinky finger on that hand twice to cycle to the high-explosive penetrating rounds—charges designed to burrow their way through the building walls and then explode only when within at most two meters of the target. Unlike the shaped penetration rockets she and her squad had used at the café the day before, these were wide area effect rounds that used their own shrapnel instead of just a shaped charge to doubly ensure the target's death.

Unfortunately, the tiny computer brain in each round simply didn't care about the innocent civilians standing around the target, and they would be just as dead from the blast. On top of that, a single HE round used on a building this small and poorly constructed was overkill and would be as likely to take out everyone on the same floor as the target and possibly some of those on the floors immediately above and below.

Sarah took a deep breath, steeling herself against the pain that resurfaced as she continued to hesitate; the agony quickly built to the level of someone shoving an ice pick through her temple. She was about to twitch her index finger and send the round to its destination (and to her blessed relief) when she noticed something in her HUD. One of the thermal readings... *Is that a...?*

She relaxed her index finger and started to lower her arm, but instantly, the pain in her head doubled, and she slumped in the suit's embrace, this time with an audible choking gasp. She couldn't remember the last time she'd felt the pain this badly, and it threatened to overwhelm her senses. At the same time, her subconscious obedience response tried to take over and lift her arm back to discharge the missile. She fought the unbearable urge and physically forced her arm down lower and off target.

"Sir," she practically whimpered through teeth gritted against the pain. "One of the civilians is an infant. The suit calculates a 91 percent probability of the child's death given its proximity to the target."

There was silence on her comm for a long moment as the pain continued to build and sharpen beyond what Sarah had even imagined was possible. Without conscious thought, she screamed, not caring if Sandoval heard her. The sound reverberated inside the small cockpit dome, assaulting senses already overloaded by her physical anguish. But over and over again, she heard Tavi's voice: 'If you knew it was wrong, would you still do it?'

"Tavi, no. I can't," she sputtered through the tears streaming down her face. "Geneva, I can't. I just can't!" She didn't care that Sandoval and anyone else in the CP could hear her desperate pleas; she wasn't even thinking about her officers anymore.

The pain continued to strengthen measure by agonizing measure, and Sarah felt consciousness slipping away from her. From stories at the Academy, she knew there was a point beyond consciousness where her subconscious brain would take complete control and enact her orders just to make the pain stop. She couldn't let that happen, so she shook her head violently to keep herself awake. Lights flashed through lids closed tightly as her suit and HUD desperately tried to make sense of her head movement and panicked facial expressions.

Finally, after what seemed like an eternity in the throes of agony,

Sandoval spoke, and even through the pain, Sarah registered the frustration in his voice. "Nowak, you have your orders. Execute now!"

Sarah felt the pain double again, then triple, though those concepts had lost all meaning in the desperate fight with her own mind. Images flashed through her head of her baby girl at home, and she saw in her mind's eye the look of horror on Tavi's face if she ever told him she'd killed an infant, even under strict orders. But now, it wasn't some nameless, faceless Panamarian baby she imagined in that doomed building; it was her daughter Geneva!

She fell to one knee, the suit shaking the surrounding ground with the impact. "Nowak, report!" yelled Sandoval through the comm, but she ignored him. Her teeth were grinding, and she squeezed her eyes more tightly shut, but tears still streamed unabated down her face. She screamed again, and the noise rebounded around the enclosed bubble of the suit. It felt now like a dozen knives were being thrust into her skull and twisted and moved around to turn her brain into goulash. The pain had spread from her head, and she felt the muscles in her back and legs spasm as her entire body writhed in the confines of the suit.

Sarah kept seeing the rotating images of Geneva playing on her lap and Tavi asking her if she'd ever had to do something she knew was wrong to follow orders. The images and words rotated faster and faster through her mind while the voice of Lieutenant Sandoval called out in impotent frustration to her through the horror of the pain.

Slowly, inexorably, her left arm raised back up, and her left eye twitched open as she felt her consciousness fade and her subconscious brain took control of her body for the simple expedient of reducing the pain. "No!" she screamed. "I won't!"

Miraculously, through the confusion of her face's agony-driven convulsions, her HUD had cycled back to the thermal view. Now she could see again the baby outlined in the blue designating it as a civilian, held by a larger thermal image of an adult, probably its mother. Less than two meters away was the yellow-outlined, flashing image of Sarah's target.

Her left arm raised higher, and Sarah knew with a terror apart from the physical pain she felt, that in mere fractions of a second, she would follow her orders regardless of her battle against them.

Forcing down the pain into a small place in her mind she hadn't known existed and summoning the last of her strength, she barely managed to twitch the fingers of her right hand in a moderately complicated sequence that overrode one of the suit's core programming imperatives. Her left arm continued to rise of its own volition, but she fought hard enough to alter its trajectory just so.

"Geneva," she cried, "Tavi, forgive me." Then Sarah's left index finger twitched once.

NINE
RECORDINGS
PRIVATE FENG CHU HUA, GPF

Chu Hua kept one eye on her HUD, which showed a top-down map view of the city with a green dot representing Sarah engaging the three red dots representing the rebels she'd encountered. The other eye she kept on the street in front of her, wary of potential ambushes. It was a favorite tactic of the Panamarian rebels to try and lure mechs out of position by engaging on one side while trying to maneuver heavy weapons on the other to take them out. But so far, her suit hadn't detected anything, much less any weapons large enough to do her damage. Still, it paid to be...

"Nowak is down! Repeat. Nowak is down!" The lieutenant's voice cut through the comm channel, and Chu Hua felt a moment of panic. Thus far, the Guard had lost only a couple of mechs on Panamar. And the thought that Sarah Nowak, one of the best mech drivers in the platoon, if not the whole division, could be down...it couldn't be!

Without thinking or waiting for further orders, Feng pivoted her mech and started sprinting down an alleyway that connected her assigned avenue to Sarah's. In her panic to reach her friend, her eyes were on her HUD's map, showing a flashing orange dot where Sargeant Nowak's green dot had previously been, and she didn't even see the wall that bisected the alley until her mech was already barreling through the crumbling local brick. Before she could react, her suit came to an abrupt and painful stop, a metallic ringing echoing through her dome. She'd run headlong into a dumpster on the other side of the thin wall!

Luckily, her mech was still in one piece; it would take much more than a collision like that to damage the thing, aside from scratching the paint here and there. So, she got back up and continued running toward her friend, every step of the massive machine buckling the pavement underneath it and shaking the surrounding buildings.

There! She saw a downed mech up ahead as she turned the corner onto the other avenue. It looked fine from her angle, but it was lying on the street with its massive feet toward her, so she couldn't see the dome. She sprinted hard, reaching more than thirty km/h in the short straightaway, and forgot to slow down in time, overshooting Nowak's downed suit as she tried to stop her massive machine.

She whirled and backtracked to her friend, but now she could see the shattered dome of the downed mech, and the blood that shown a brighter shade of red than the crimson light all around it. But she could only see the back of Sarah's head through the gore. Grunting and making full use of her suit's tremendous strength, she reached down and turned over her friend's fallen suit. Then she gasped as she saw that half of Sarah's head was just gone. The one remaining eye stared up vacantly at a spot in the sky.

Chu Hua stopped, holding her breath in stunned disbelief. Sarah was dead! Her HUD had told her that, of course, before she'd even started her mad dash to her sergeant's side, but seeing it now, in person, somehow made it real.

Tears rushed to her eyes as she fell forward, letting her mech crash to its knees next to Sarah's. "Sarah, no," she whimpered.

Through the fog of shock and despair, a single lucid thought occurred to her. She had to know what happened. She twitched her nose and stuck out her tongue in a pattern her suit recognized and then watched as the words she hoped for flashed onto her HUD.

Suit connection established. Terminal sequence download initiated.

While the download finished, her thoughts flashed to Octavio and Geneva. Their wife and mother was just... gone. And she was never coming back. Feng sobbed anew, and then her HUD flashed a message that it had finished downloading the last few minutes of recordings from Sarah's suit.

She played the video, kneeling there next to her dead friend, and gasped. She saw first the part where Sarah had driven one of the three rebels, the only survivor of her initial attack, into a nearby apartment building. Then she heard the discussion between Sarah and Sandoval about how to take the guy out, ending with the lieutenant's order to hit the rebel through the building walls with a high explosive penetrator round. And she heard Nowak's gasping argument when she saw the thermal outline of a mother with an infant inside the blast radius.

From there, the vid got shaky as Sarah not only disobeyed the order but then brought her suit's own arm up to put a penetrator round right through her mech's dome and into her head, gasping out a plea for forgiveness to Octavio and Geneva with her last dying breath.

She disobeyed a direct order! Chu Hua thought in amazement. *That's not supposed to be possible.* The rebels hadn't taken Sarah out! She'd killed herself just to stop herself from following an order!

The horror of that realization faded quickly as the reason for Sarah's suicide sunk in. Sandoval had ordered her to take out a building full of civilians to kill just one young rebel soldier who had fled inside. And one of those civilians had been a small child...a baby.

A baby! How could they order her to kill a baby? She's a new mother, and they ordered her to kill a baby? For one measly rebel?

In that moment, facing the horrible truth, Private Feng Chu Hua changed forever in a fundamental way that she'd never imagined was possible.

TEN
DESERTER
PRIVATE FENG CHU HUA, GPF

Later that evening, the sentries at the base's edge hadn't even challenged Feng as she'd walked out of the Guard camp and into the short stretch of jungle that separated the forward operating base from the edge of San Sebastian. One of them had looked like he might ask where she was going, but then he'd clearly seen the Mech patch on her uniform and stopped himself. After all, only enacters drove mechs, and no enacter would—could—ever desert, right?

Luckily, he didn't come closer, or he might have seen the sweat soaking into Chu Hua's uniform that went far beyond the norm for even this jungle hell of a planet. Or he might have seen the pained grimace she could barely hide.

Once, way back in the Academy, Chu Hua had tried her best to disobey a simple order just to see what would happen. The result had been an agony beyond what she'd ever dared to expect, as her enacter gene triggered her body's pain response in increasingly devastating waves the longer she waited to obey the order. She'd quickly abandoned her experiment and vowed to herself that she would never go through that kind of ordeal ever again.

But now, here she was, not only disobeying orders but actually deserting her post! And the pain was excruciating, so bad that she could barely walk upright. The feeling of an ice pick penetrating each temple and being used to stir up her brain matter was so much worse than even what she'd experienced that one night at the Academy, and every step felt like a kilometer.

Still, every time her body and mind screamed at her to turn back and make the pain stop, Chu Hua pictured her friend, Sarah, bouncing Geneva on her knee a few nights before deployment and promising her daughter and her husband that she'd come home to them.

Which she hadn't because she had disobeyed an immoral and terrible order. Could Feng do any less to honor the memory of her friend? Besides, hadn't the order itself, along with the general resistance of the civilian population on this horrid little planet, decisively shown that the Guard weren't the good guys here?

Even those thoughts didn't quell the pain, but they did somehow make the alternative seem worse. There was no way she could stay and simply continue to follow orders, not after what had happened to her mentor and friend. So, the way she saw it, she had only two choices: escape and deal with the pain, or put an end to it...forever. A hundred times in the first kilometer she walked from the base, she almost drew her service sidearm to take the second choice, but something kept her going, one foot after another, until there was nothing but the pain.

She quickly lost track of the distance and even direction she traveled, both becoming nothing more than abstract concepts in her muddled brain, everything else fading to the background as she wrestled with the pain.

Soon, she forgot nearly *everything* but the pain, even her own name. She forgot why she was walking the way she was, and several times, almost surrendered to the overwhelming subconscious impulse to turn around—to walk back the way she'd come because somehow she *knew* that would end the pain.

But she kept going: one foot in front of the next, a little more pain with each excruciating step, until even the increases became immeasurable to her tortured mind.

And even though she couldn't remember her own name, she remembered another: Sarah. It was Sarah's face, shattered and broken inside her mech, that kept reappearing to her…that kept her walking despite the growing agony.

Chu Hua came back to herself as darkness fell. She found herself in a bombed-out section of the city that she vaguely recognized from some of her unit's earliest operations on the planet. And knowing that she had almost nothing left in her, she looked for shelter.

Coming back to full consciousness brought the pain roaring back with a vengeance, and she almost turned around to march right back to the base and her barracks. But she forced one step, then another, again, telling herself that there were only a few more meters to go.

Five meters short of one of the buildings, her legs gave out, and she fell to the ground, laying there for a long moment, face down, every centimeter of her screaming that it was time to go back, turn herself in, and face the consequences—anything to make the pain stop!

Finding a wellspring of energy that she couldn't define, she crawled forward, thoughts of Sarah's final moments fueling her rage against the pain. And as her anger and her agony met, they battled for her very soul. A few minutes later, she found herself in what looked like an old first-floor apartment living room, one corner of it open to the sky and the street. On one side was a debris-covered couch that beckoned her to go and lie down and grapple with the pain in some semblance of comfort. But she shied away from that, knowing somehow that even a moment of false comfort would degrade her final defensive walls and have her running back to the base.

So, instead, she crawled to the room's other side, where a sturdy-looking dining table wrought of local wood and iron sat, cracked in half. Reaching it, she pulled the handcuffs from her pocket that she'd brought for this very purpose, affixing one end to her wrist and the other to one of the decorative iron circles attached to the bottom of the table. Testing it to make sure it would hold her, she painfully grasped the key from that same pocket and threw it across the room and out of her reach.

Then, Feng Chu Hua screamed, a primal sound that conveyed the pain, the anger, and the frustration that boiled inside her. She screamed, and she screamed, over and over again, until exhausted sleep finally took her.

The sound of something falling snapped Chu Hua back to wakefulness. Her first thought upon waking was that the pain hadn't receded. It was still there, churning its way through her brain and shouting at her to just follow orders to make it go away. Yet, surprisingly, though the pain didn't seem to have lessened one bit, it somehow felt...distant.

She couldn't explain it or even describe it to herself, but it was almost as if the pain were assaulting someone else, and Chu Hua herself was just an observer. She could still feel it, but she wasn't experiencing it the same way she had the night before.

Another sound broke off her thoughts in that direction, and she looked up to see the source, her free hand going to the pistol at her belt and pulling it out to point at the doorway from which the sound seemed to have emanated.

The noise of a hesitant step in the hall right outside the open doorway made Chu Hua tighten her finger on the trigger. A figure came into view, and she prepared to squeeze off a shot; her gun was set to fire lethal projectiles—she intrinsically knew that the people coming after her wouldn't bother with stun shots, and neither should she.

But the figure was all wrong for a Guard kill or capture team. Instead of a Guard reg in body armor, the person in the doorway was a girl who couldn't have been over ten years old.

The girl's eyes went wide upon seeing Feng lying by the table, and then she took a frantic step back when she saw the pistol pointed at her head. Chu Hua maintained the presence of mind to quickly lower the weapon and even put it back in her belt holster, then held up her now empty hand, the one that wasn't cuffed to the table.

The girl studied her for a moment, taking a timid step back into the room. She cocked her head and seemed to be thinking hard about what to do. Then she lifted one of her hands and gave a shy wave.

Chu Hua, taken aback by the simple gesture, awkwardly waved back. Despite the pain still pounding in her head, she even managed a smile at the little girl.

The girl smiled back, then turned and looked back the way she'd come. "Mamá!" she called out, cupping her hands to her mouth to help her voice carry. She followed it with a string of words in a language that Chu Hua vaguely recognized as the Italio-Portuguese that most of the Panamarians in the capital of San Sebastian spoke.

The sound of a new set of footsteps came from the hallway, and Feng tensed again, her right hand twitching back down to her pistol at her belt before she stopped it. The girl looked back at her and smiled. If it was an ambush, it was sure a friendly one.

Another figure appeared in the doorway behind the little girl, a woman who looked to be in her forties, with a black scarf over her head and brown hair peeking out from underneath it. She studied Feng from over the girl's shoulder, but when the woman's eyes moved down from Feng's face and saw the Guard uniform, she abruptly cried out and pushed the girl behind her, her hands held out in a warding gesture. She started backing up, chattering in the same language the girl had used and using her body to push the little girl out of the doorway and back into the relative safety of the hall.

"Wait!" Chu Hua cried ahead of any conscious thought.

Perhaps it was the desperation in her voice, so different from the commanding tone the woman may have expected from a guardswoman, or maybe it was the fact that Feng hadn't pulled her weapon again. Either way, the woman stopped and furrowed her eyebrows, clearly confused.

"English?" Chu Hua asked hopefully. Had she had her watch, she could have used its built-in translator to have an easy conversation with the woman, but it also would have told her commanding officer and any other member of the Guard exactly where Feng was. She had left it back in her bunk.

The woman's eyes shot up, and she cocked her head to the side, her eyes going to Feng's empty hands and lingering on the one cuffed to the table. But she said nothing to Chu Hua's question.

"I speak English," a small voice said, and the head of the little girl poked out from around her mother's back.

Feng let go of a sigh of relief. "I...uh." She wasn't sure what to even say now that she could communicate with the two natives; her brain was completely blank.

"You are Guard?" the little girl asked, pointing toward Chu Hua's uniform.

"Yes—I mean no!" Feng answered hastily. "I mean, I was, but I...left."

The girl looked confused at this but looked up at her mother and rattled off words in Italio-Portuguese, hopefully translating what Feng had said.

The mother looked at her daughter and said something.

"My mother wants to know if you are here to arrest us," the girl said, with eyes going wide with a measure of fear.

"No! I'm not going to arrest you," Feng answered quickly, holding up her free hand to show she still wasn't holding a weapon. "I need help. I deserted." The girl looked confused at the word. "I ran away," Feng repeated. "The Guard is after me now, too."

The girl's eyes stayed wide as she repeated the story back to her mother. The mother's eyes went equally wide, and she rattled something off to her daughter.

The girl looked back at Feng with a broad smile. "You come with us now."

Communicating through the little girl, Feng was able to guide the mother to find the key to the cuffs where she had thrown it. The woman had kept her eyes on the gun on Chu Hua's belt the entire time, prompting Feng to slowly remove it and toss it across the room and onto the couch before the woman would unlock her.

As soon as the cuff was removed, a wave of pain came roaring back, knocking her to the ground from where she'd started to get up to follow the mother and daughter. She screamed at the unexpected sharp spike of agony, and the mother shied away, putting her body between Chu Hua and her daughter. But the pain passed, and Chu Hua was able to communicate through gasping breaths that she was all right.

She followed the woman and the young girl from the room, leaving the gun behind where she'd tossed it.

The next few days were a blur. The mother and daughter that found Chu Hua had taken her back to what she guessed was their apartment, in a building that seemed to have mostly escaped damage from the fighting. There, and at her urging, they handcuffed her to one of the beds in a small room that looked like it may have belonged to a small boy at one point but no longer seemed lived in.

For the next few days and nights, Chu Hua alternated between writhing and screaming in agony—she had them gag her so no one could hear her and tie up her other hand so she couldn't remove the gag and call for help—and troubled fitful sleep. The mother tried to give her food and water a few times, but beyond a few sips of water, Chu Hua hadn't been able to keep anything down.

Finally, on the fourth day, she awoke to find the pain in her head distant but strangely faded. It was still there, to be sure, but it was far more manageable than before. Chu Hua wasn't sure if that was because the pain itself had actually lessened or that her body and mind were somehow adapting to it. She didn't care either way and for the first time, she was able to allow the mother to untie her uncuffed hand and help her eat some watery soup.

A day later, they uncuffed her, and though the pain came back somewhat at her subconsciousness' realization that she could move now and return to the base if she wanted to, it was still bearable.

It was two days after that that the men arrived to take her away.

PART TWO
PATEL

ELEVEN
TRIAL
BOHDI PATEL

TEN YEARS AGO – 721 P.D.

"In the case of the Council versus Patel..." The judge's voice didn't even try to hide the man's boredom as he squinted at the holo display that only he could see. The courtroom was empty except for a few members of the Barristers Corps, who lounged in boredom at the back of the room. None of those lawyers were helping Bohdi Patel; they cost way more than his parents could afford. In fact, his parents hadn't even been able to make it from their small farm in the southern hemisphere to support their only child in his trial. All of their spare money had been used up just to get him to Landing City in the first place.

The judge found what he was looking for and cleared his throat loudly, not looking up from the holo field as he spoke. "In the case of the Council versus Patel, I affirm the Guard's finding of the defendant's guilt on the charge of grand theft auto and approve the Prefecture's petition to try him as an adult. I hereby sentence Mr. Patel to six years in the minimum-security prison at Gentryville. A few years working in the Council textile factory there will teach you not to break the law." He smacked the dais in front of him with a gavel to punctuate the end of hope for Bohdi Patel.

The boy's heart sank deeper than he'd ever felt it go. It had been so stupid, and, as with most stupid things, it started with a girl. He hadn't even known her name, but she'd had legs that had gone for kilometers and a smile that could launch a shuttle into orbit. And she'd looked at Bohdi with such...disgust when he'd tried to go and talk to her, his friends snickering in the background and egging him on. All she'd seen when she looked at Bohdi was his worn pair of pants and his calloused hands, dirty and rough from working on his parents' farm for his entire life—all seventeen years of it. But she was the most gorgeous creature he'd ever laid eyes on, in her short dress and high-heeled shoes. So, he wasn't going to give up that easily.

He hadn't really been going to steal the hovercar, but the driver had left it running when she'd run into a store. And it had been so pretty and red, not like anything they had back home in the Southlands. Bohdi was only going to borrow it just to drive past the pretty girl and her friends at their table at the outdoor cafe. He'd rehearsed it in his head. He would pull to the side of the road and throw the girl a wink. She would be impressed by the shiny red sports car, and he would hit the accelerator and swerve around the corner. Then he'd return the car to exactly where he found it before the owner was any the wiser and walk back on foot to talk to the girl. At that point, she would be smitten and ready to throw herself at him! It was foolproof.

How was he supposed to know the car would have a biometric lock? Once he'd gotten inside and tried to put it into drive, a very impolite computerized voice had said something about him not being an authorized user and had locked him inside the car. There, he had waited in frustrated agony while his classmates laughed at him from outside. Leave it to Bohdi to get into trouble on the one and only class field trip to Landing City. Leave it to him to do something monumentally stupid.

The worst part had been that the girl had walked by with her friends, their meal at the cafe done, just at the same time as the Guard cruiser pulled up, and two burly guardsmen put Bohdi in handcuffs and threw him in the back of the squad car. She had laughed at him, too!

Apparently, the Guard took borrowing someone else's car pretty seriously in the big city. Instead of a slap on the wrist, they'd thrown him in jail! He'd been there a full week, with only a single comm call to his distraught parents and a visit from his frustrated teacher before they finally brought him in front of this judge. Bohdi had actually practiced what he would tell the judge, but the man hadn't even let him speak beyond giving his name and identification number. And now they were putting him in prison for six years! For borrowing a car?

"Your honor," Bohdi said, trying to sound apologetic, just like he'd practiced in his cell. "I'm real sorry. I didn't mean to cause any trouble. I wasn't going to steal that car. I swear. Can't I just go home to my family and work on their farm? They need me there. I'll never come back to Landing, I promise." It sounded lame even to him.

The judge frowned and looked down at him as if noticing Bohdi for the first time despite having just pronounced the sentence that would destroy his life. Then the man's eyebrows went up, and he smirked. "Farm work, huh? Say, you're a rather strong-looking lad, aren't you?"

Bohdi was confused. What did that have to do with anything?

The judge didn't wait for a response but continued talking. "Good pair of shoulders. Tall enough. Fire in your eyes. And you're seventeen. Not technically old enough, but you'll be eighteen in what..." he consulted the holo in front of him, "...two months? Close enough."

He looked over at the court recorder, who took down all of the decisions and sentences handed out in the courtroom, and the judge smiled in a way that Bohdi really didn't like.

"Strike that five years in Gentryville from the record, Nia. This one's going to the GPF. They're a bit low on their quota this month. Boy like this should make fine fodder for the infantry."

He looked back at Bohdi with a wicked grin. "Five years minimum with the Guard Paramilitary Force. You'll be on the first transport to Cigni II. And you're welcome!" The gavel fell again, and Bohdi was dragged out of the courtroom in stunned silence by an overweight bailiff who was laughing at him just like that pretty girl.

TWELVE
THE ASTEROID
LIEUTENANT BOHDI PATEL, GPF

EIGHTEEN MONTHS AGO – 730 P.D.

Lieutenant Bohdi Patel wished he could wipe the sweat off his brow, but the vac-sealed helmet he wore prevented that. Instead, he had to just let it drip into his eyes and make them sting like crazy.

You would think someone would have invented something to stop that by now, he thought morosely, though he knew someone likely had. Only the GPF hadn't seen fit to spend the money to outfit its ground forces with anything aimed at their comfort in combat.

He shook off the semi-treasonous thought, thankful for the millionth time or more that he wasn't an enacter and could have those types of thoughts without a severe headache to follow. But instead of dwelling on his hatred for GPF bean counters, he looked across the crater at the long, two-story miners' barracks building that occupied the other side, the steady light of the Mako system's primary so small behind the building that it looked like just another star in the night sky.

On the surface, nothing looked amiss in the barracks building. But he knew that inside were almost two hundred miners and at least one senior management trainee they'd taken hostage. Supposedly, the miners were demanding four million credits for the woman's safe release, but that was all way above Bohdi's head. All he knew was that Captain Nigel Houseman, his direct GPF superior, had decided it was time to call the miners' bluff. And Bohdi and his 3rd Platoon got to be the pointy end of the spear to get the poor woman back.

"Listen up folks!" barked Houseman's voice through Bohdi's helmet comm on an open channel to the entirety of Fox Company. "Third Platoon goes in first, hard and fast and right down the middle. Second and 1st will circle around the crater and hit the building from both ends. Any questions?"

There were none. Only Fox Company's three lieutenants would dare ask the captain a question at a time like this, and they had already been thoroughly briefed and had their limited opportunity to suggest changes to the plan, none of which Houseman took.

"OK, we go on my mark," the captain continued. "Mark!"

"Go! Go! Go!" Bohdi yelled over his platoon's comm channel, and all three squads—thirty-six men and women—of 3rd Platoon leapt forward. Not wanting to be exposed for the long moments it would take the asteroid's slight gravity to pull them to the bottom of the five-meter-deep crater, they all fired their shoulder thrusters to push them to the bottom, which they hit running, continuously firing the thrusters just enough to simulate something approaching 1g. Then, as soon as they hit the lowest point of the crater, they collectively cut their thrusters and started to bound up the steep opposite side of the crater, just under the edge of their target building.

In all, it took less than ten seconds for the first elements of 3rd Platoon, 1st Squad, to reach the top of the crater and plant themselves on the two-meter-wide expanse of rock that separated the edge from the building's outer wall. Without waiting for further orders from Bohdi, Sergeant Linus directed her demo expert, Corporal Balakirev, to place the shaped explosive on the building's reinforced concrete side while the rest of 1st Squad covered him, rifles pointed at the nearby windows.

Luckily, there was no enemy fire. Intel said that the miners had only a few guns between all of them but were armed with a couple of mining lasers they'd stolen from the mine, along with various other industrial tools that could do some real damage.

The explosive set, 1st Squad moved back to the crater's edge and dropped below it, where the rest of 3rd Platoon waited for them.

"Blow it," Bohdi commanded as soon as he verified all of his troops were safe below the lip of the crater. He didn't hear the explosion—the asteroid's gravity was far too little to maintain any atmosphere, but he did see the dust that it kicked up. "Go!" he commanded again and reached up to grab the crater's edge and pull himself up with the rest of his platoon.

First Squad took the lead again, Linus herself taking point through the now gaping hole in the side of the building, using her back thrusters to help her fight the flow of air rushing out from the now compromised structure. Bohdi was right behind them, followed quickly by the other two squads. He knew that he would catch flak from Houseman for not being the last through the gap, but leading from the rear had never sat well with him, so he accepted the inevitable chewing out and pushed forward.

Over the comms, he could hear 1st Squad calling out kills. Given that the miners were armed and holding a hostage, Houseman had only issued his troops kill shots. There would be no stunners on this mission.

On the command channel, Bohdi heard the reports of 1st and 2nd Platoon entering the building through its main airlocks at either end. The plan was for him to divide up his squads to search from the center of the building out while the other two platoons searched from each end in. First to find the hostage, per Houseman, would get a case of beer.

"Contact!" cried Linus in her helmet comm, pulling her attention away from what the other two platoons were doing. They'd moved on from the room they'd blown a hole in, overriding the pressure doors that had shut to minimize the loss of atmosphere, and now the entire platoon was in a section of the building that still had air. So, the sound of rail gun fire carried to Bohdi from down a narrow hallway. So did the cries of men and women, hopefully the ones on the receiving end of that fire and not any of Bohdi's troops.

He didn't have to worry. Rules of engagement were clear on this op: shoot the miners on sight. There was no way to know where their various weapons would be or who would be armed; given that they were using industrial tools, they wouldn't show up on military weapons scanners. So, Houseman had ordered all of his men and women to shoot first and sort things out later. The order had given Bohdi a strange feeling in the pit of his stomach, but according to his captain, the miners had forfeited any hope of resolving things peacefully when they'd taken a hostage. And Bohdi was at least comforted that the captain was making it easier to bring all of their people out alive by having clear rules of engagement in an otherwise ambiguous situation.

Still, he winced as he heard more gunfire and the screams of the dying. This was the first time he'd heard that sort of thing outside of combat exercises, and it made him want to stop and order his troops back. But his training took over, and he resisted the urge, using comm channels with his sergeants and his HUD map to ensure they didn't leave a single room unsearched for the hostage.

Then it happened. Bohdi was walking down a short stretch of hallway that had already been cleared of enemies, moving forward to check on 3rd Squad's possible sighting of the hostage, when a figure leapt out of a doorway to his right. Again, his training took over, and he swung his own assault rifle toward the wild bearded man who had something in his hand raised high overhead.

Bohdi pulled the trigger, and the man was instantly knocked to the ground, falling back inside the room he'd emerged from. Shaking with adrenaline, Bohdi moved into the room after him, eyes scanning for additional threats. He saw none and turned his gaze back down to the man he'd shot.

He was shocked to see that the 'man' wasn't even as old as Bohdi. In fact, he looked several years younger, maybe still a teenager. His face was covered in a scraggly beard, above which his eyes were still open wide but now unseeing. Suddenly, Bohdi felt sick to his stomach, and he started to frantically search for the weapon he'd seen in the boy's hand. When he saw it, he had to rip his helmet off just in time to lose his breakfast in the corner of the room.

The boy had leapt at him brandishing what was apparently the only weapon available to him. A rock. Nothing more than a small gray rock that was undoubtedly picked up on one of his forays into the asteroid's mines. A rock that wasn't even large enough or heavy enough to have done more than scratch the transparent dome of Bohdi's helmet.

But, unfortunately for the boy, the railgun round that Bohdi had fired had been far more deadly. The boy's chest now featured a gaping hole where the hollow round—designed for use in pressurized environments where shooting through a wall could create an atmospheric breach—had hit and instantly expanded. He'd been dead before he even hit the ground.

"You OK, Eltee?" a voice said from the doorway behind Bohdi, and he looked up and around from where he'd puked all over the floor and part of a wall to see Corporal Evers looking at him in mixed concern and embarrassment. "Sarge sent me back to bring you forward," the boy explained, trying very hard not to look at the remnants of Bohdi's last meal.

"Uh, sure, Evers," Bohdi said through the sour taste in his mouth. "Just..."

For a moment, Evers looked like he might fill in the rest of Bohdi's unfinished sentence, but then the boy looked down at the young dead miner and physically shivered himself. "Yes, sir," he said simply, and that was enough.

Twenty minutes later, the command channel carried the news that all rooms had been cleared and that all the rebel miners were either dead, injured, or—for the lucky few allowed to do so—had surrendered. But the rumored mining lasers they'd stolen hadn't been found. Nor had the hostage.

They did eventually find the 'hostage' two hours later, in a supply closet back in the management building. She'd passed out there drunk after a night with her friends, and magically, no one could recall just where they'd heard she'd been taken hostage by the miners. It was a mystery.

Except it wasn't. Because Bohdi Patel was pretty sure he knew exactly what had happened. Houseman hadn't cared if the woman was a hostage or not; he had simply used the fact she was missing as the pretense he needed to take out the rebel miners, who, it turned out, hadn't really been armed or even expecting a fight. They had only been holed up in their barracks, refusing to return to work until the mining company agreed to negotiate in good faith on a salary increase. There had never been a hostage, and Bohdi suspected there had never been a demand for four million credits as ransom or otherwise.

Based on what he pieced together later, 129 miners were dead as an example to the other 524 on the asteroid, all so the mining company didn't have to pay any of them a ten-percent raise.

Still, Bohdi said nothing. Because he was convinced it wouldn't do any good at all.

THIRTEEN
ROOMMATES
CAPTAIN BOHDI PATEL, GPF

PRESENT DAY

Captain Bohdi Patel walked into the officers' mess in the Guard 3rd Infantry Division headquarters camp outside of San Sebastian, Panamar. As a company commander, he split his time between the infantry HQ and the main forward operating base just south of the city, but today, he was gratified to be back 'home' and away from the stomping mech drivers always coming and going from the FOB.

He had just spent the last twelve hours in the field, observing the operations of his company in the thick of the fighting in the city's southeastern sector, and he was more than exhausted. Though he felt bad even complaining about the aches and pains he had; after all, he'd spent at least half the day riding in an uncomfortable armored command hovercar while the men and women under his command had been on foot, taking only rare breaks to rest or eat throughout the day.

He was late for chow, so the line at the food counter was blessedly short. As he walked toward it, his face lit up as he recognized the man at the back of the line.

"Sandy? When did they let a mech gorilla like you into the camp?"

The man he was addressing turned to reveal the short stature, dark hair, and olive skin of a man roughly the same age as Patel himself. But despite the warmth of Bohdi's greeting, the man did not smile or show any other sign of good humor.

"Oh, it's you, Bohdi," Jose Sandoval—'Sandy' for short—said in a morose tone that instantly took the smile off Patel's face. He and Bohdi had been roommates in their final year at the Guard Paramilitary Officers Candidate's School on Centauri IV before Sandoval had left for Greater York and mech training, and Patel had gone straight into his first deployment on Sinai in the Coreward Rim.

They had gotten along pretty well at OCS, despite one being an enacter and the other being the headstrong son of farmers who had joined the Guard more as a way to avoid prison than out of any real desire to serve the Council. And whereas Bohdi had questioned everything he'd learned, first at the Guard Academy and then at OCS, Sandoval had had a reputation of being strictly by-the-book, even for an enacter. When his roommate would occasionally sneak out at night for a drink at a local bar or the rare romantic liaison, Jose would always stay back in their room, studying and doing whatever else he thought was necessary to please the instructors.

Despite all of that, the two had become friends. Though Patel had had no luck in changing the taciturn and rigid Sandoval during their time together. He understood, of course, that the man was an enacter and couldn't question orders or even the Council's wisdom. But he was also completely unimaginative, never finding new or interesting ways to solve the tactical problems presented to them; rather, he had always gone strictly by what regulations or training manuals said was the best solution. It had earned him solid passing grades, if not anything more.

Even back then, Bohdi knew that his friend would never advance as far as he hoped in the hierarchy of the Guard. He would be terrific at taking orders and passing them along to his troops but never at making the tough decisions on the ground without guidance from his direct superiors or the operational manuals. It was no doubt why he remained a lowly first lieutenant in the mechanized divisions while Bohdi and most of the rest of their graduating class had already made Captain or above.

Still, seeing his friend had brought a smile to Patel's face after such a grueling day, but that smile was gone now that he saw his friend's sullen countenance.

"What's up, buddy?" he asked, pitching his voice low so that others in the mess hall wouldn't hear their conversation as they moved through the food line.

Jose frowned as if trying to decide how to respond and not liking any of his options. Finally, he shrugged. "Nothing much, I suppose."

Bohdi didn't buy the answer for an instant but played along, knowing that he would have to draw out the truth slowly from the other man. "So, why are you here, slumming it with the regs?" The lame attempt at humor elicited no reaction from the short mech officer.

Sandoval shrugged again. "I'm here because General Ostertag needed a runner to send a message to General Nissen, and I was available."

Bohdi frowned. It wasn't common practice to send officers as runners unless the message bore a high security risk and couldn't be entrusted to an enlisted man. And that was even rarer for a division of enacters where even the lowliest private could be absolutely trusted to follow their orders to the letter and never reveal sensitive information willingly. Something had to have happened to make the general of the entire mechanized division tap a lieutenant to carry a simple message and, judging by his friend's morose look, that something hadn't been good for Jose Sandoval.

They had reached the front of the line and stopped talking to gather their food onto their trays, and Jose walked away to find a table without a word. Bohdi shrugged mentally and followed after him without an invitation, sitting across from him at an empty table in the far corner, away from the smattering of officers that were still in the mess hall this late.

They sat in silence for a few minutes, Bohdi, despite his curiosity, shoveling food into his mouth—he was starving after the combat-filled day—while Jose picked at his food with his fork and mostly just moved it around his plate, refusing to meet his friend's eyes.

Finally, the edge of his hunger satisfied, Patel set down his fork and looked at his friend with raised eyebrows. "So, seriously, buddy, tell me what's going on. You look like my sister did after my dad killed her favorite cow." Bohdi hadn't been on a farm in over a decade, except for brief visits home, but still liked to use colloquialisms and metaphors as if he'd left it the day before. It disarmed others and fooled them into thinking he was a dumb country hick rather than an accomplished Guard paramilitary officer who was on the fast track to Major and beyond. Usually, his farm humor could get even the overly serious Jose to crack a smile, but not this time. Still, he waited patiently for his taciturn friend to respond.

Finally, Sandoval looked up and frowned at him. "It's nothing. I can't talk about it." But his eyes were wide and pleading.

Bohdi frowned. His friend obviously wanted desperately to talk about whatever was bothering him but felt he couldn't, probably because someone had ordered him not to, and he was an obedient little enacter, after all. The good news was that Patel had cracked the code of Jose Sandoval and his enacter gene years ago at OCS and knew that the man's strict, genetically enforced obedience wasn't the impenetrable wall that the Council and the Guard would have everyone believe. Getting the information from his friend that he so badly needed to get off his chest wouldn't be easy, but Bohdi knew how to play the game.

"Alright," he started, "so don't tell me. I understand. But can I ask you a question?"

Sandoval nodded, a glimmer of hope passing briefly across his features as he recognized what his friend was trying to do. But then he winced in pain, no doubt because he wanted Patel to succeed in his quest for information, and his subconscious was punishing him for even considering disobedience. *I'll have to tread lighter than usual*, Bohdi thought.

"Was being sent here as a messenger a good thing for you?"

Sandoval considered the question for a long moment, rolling over potential answers in his head. Finally, he looked back up at his friend and shrugged again. "Not necessarily."

Got it. Have to keep digging, Bohdi thought. "Was it a punishment?"

"Not officially, no."

So definitely a punishment. "Were you chosen for the duty specifically by General Ostertag or by another junior officer?"

"The general himself ordered that it be me who would bring the message here."

Bohdi sat back, surprised. If Ostertag himself had descended from his throne on high to assign punitive messenger duty to a lowly lieutenant, one of hundreds under his command, then things must be truly bad for his friend. He considered his next question carefully. "Did you personally do something wrong, or someone in your platoon?"

Jose winced, and Patel immediately knew he'd pushed too hard too quickly. It was obviously hurting the man to even consider the answer to that question. But to his credit, the small mech officer shook off the pain and answered him. "I did nothing wrong."

OK, so that means it was someone in his platoon, most likely. But what possible trouble could a platoon full of enacters get themselves into that would be bad enough to upset a Major General? "How are things in the camp?" he asked, changing the angle of his questioning.

Jose smiled slightly, then quickly winced again. "They're OK, just like things in the field, I suppose."

Bohdi raised his eyebrows. He had expected the man to either answer that things in the camp were fine, indicating that the problem was in the combat area, or to answer that things in the camp weren't all that great, conveying that whatever had gotten him in trouble had happened there. But the way he answered the question suggested a problem that was both in the camp and in the field.

Sandoval continued to wince in pain, and Bohdi knew he had pushed the man just about as far as he could before he would shut down completely to avoid the agony of disobedience. His friend Sandy had always seemed to have a pretty low pain threshold, even for an enacter. *So, it's time to go for broke,* he thought. *I'll get maybe one last question at best.* "You know," he started, his voice as casual as he could make it. "There's this nasty rumor circulating in the camp that one, or maybe even two mechies may have disobeyed their orders—one may have even offed themselves with their own mech in view of a couple of regs. Of course, I know that can't be true, them being enacters and all, but what do you think of those rumors?"

Jose's face scrunched in pain worse than before, and the man reached up to grasp the sides of his head with both hands. "R-ridiculous," he ground out through clenched teeth. "Rumors like that can't be repeated. For the good of the Guard and the Council."

Gotcha! Bohdi's inner monologue would have taken on a tone of satisfaction if not for the obvious pain that his friend was experiencing, though now that the man had answered in the negative, that pain was clearly abating. Which meant, of course, that his nasty little subconscious wouldn't have let him answer that question any differently, but that he had *wanted* to answer it differently. And that, of course, meant that Jose had been specifically ordered not to answer that very question in the affirmative.

"Makes sense. Anything more we need to talk about, Jose?" he asked the man.

Sandoval shook his head, a small smile forming on his face. *So, the enacter mechies who disobeyed were in Sandy's platoon. No wonder Ostertag is so upset with him.*

But any momentary satisfaction Patel might have felt at getting the truth, despite his friend's pain, fled as the full import of what he had just learned sunk in. *By the Council,* he thought in alarm, *the rumors are true!* One, or maybe even two enacters disobeyed their orders. That wasn't supposed to be possible. Because despite trying very hard to get Sandoval to loosen up during their time together in OCS, Bohdi Patel also knew that the very foundation of the Guard was built on one incontrovertible fact: enacters followed orders. And if that were no longer true—just like those blasted Revelations had claimed—then the Guard on Panamar and elsewhere could have a very big problem. All of a sudden, Bohdi had the mental image of a massive, two-ton, unstoppable mech going on a rampage and taking out Guard regulars and even other mechs left and right, and the daydream made him shiver in horror.

"Uh, thanks, Sandy...for the chat. It was good to see you," he said absently.

Jose Sandoval looked at his friend more intently than before, and when he spoke, his voice was a little stronger than it had been. "No, thank you, Bohdi. I enjoyed our conversation. It was good to see you, too." And it was clear that the man truly meant that, despite the pain.

PART THREE
TREASONOUS BEGINNINGS

FOURTEEN
REBEL EMISSARY
LT. COMMANDER XIN WANG, FCN

PRESENT DAY

Lieutenant Commander Xin Wang was frustrated. He was a rebel fighter pilot, a member of the ambitiously named Free Colonies Navy, not a ground pounder. But in a revolution where there were never enough trained soldiers, everyone had to play multiple roles. Especially when they were trying to stop a humanitarian and military disaster like the one in progress on Panamar.

The battle on the Edge planet between the Guard and the rebel forces had been raging for several weeks now, and the rebels were decidedly losing the battle. San Sebastian, really the only major city to speak of on the jungle hell of a planet, had almost entirely fallen to the Guard's relentless urban assault.

Xin knew the rebels were actually fairly numerous and well-equipped. Like most of the Edge worlds, Panamar had always chafed under the rule of the distant Council. And over the centuries, that chafing had often flared into actual militant resistance. Still, it had been almost a hundred years since the last time the Guard had come in force to the jungle planet to put down a semi-organized rebellion, but this time had promised to be different.

First, the rebellion actually involved many members of the Panamar Guard itself. That had only happened because, in the last two decades, Guard headquarters on New Brussels had, without explanation, sent almost none of its enacters to the planet. That had allowed an amount of freethinking in the local Guard precincts that would have scared the Council government if they'd known, but with an eight-day transit time between Panamar and New Brussels for even a simple message via fast courier ship, the exchange of information between the local precincts and HQ was lacking. And those freethinking guardmembers had slowly started to see things in a different light, in no small part due to a few relatively senior Guard officers who were actually rebel agents from the beginning and had for years been diverting portions of Guard weapons shipments to rebel stockpiles.

Second was the existence and dissemination of the Revelations. Kendra Siefred's shocking admissions about the Keeper and his plans to turn everyone in the 47 Colonies into enacters had scared a lot of people. And for a brief moment, Xin had felt soaring hope that the populace of the colonies would rise up together to cast off their autocratic masters.

But alas, his hopes were quickly dashed. For most people, the Revelations were in and out of the news cycle within a week, in no small part because the Assembly ordered them quashed, and their pet news services dutifully obeyed. But even the underground blogs never gained the traction Xin would have hoped for, not with enough people, at least. Even on worlds where the blogs had more followers, the official news services ran round-the-clock misinformation campaigns to discredit Siefred and Todd Crowley and everything they had revealed.

It was all too effective, except on the Edge. The Edge worlds, like Panamar, were so far out that the mainstream news services largely ignored them—there weren't enough paying customers for them to spend much time worrying about what was important to the Edge world dwellers. That had allowed underground blogs, despite being illegal and ostensibly hunted by the Guard, to become the de facto source of news for Panamar, Phoenix, Yukon, and Ha'ano, the edge worlds furthest from the Core. And that meant that the majority of their populations had come not only to believe the Revelations but also to start to feel anxious about throwing off the Council's authority.

So, this time around, the rebels on Panamar were better manned, better equipped, and had the support of most of the populace. And for a brief shining moment, it looked like they might triumph as the Guard was distracted putting down riots and demonstrations in the Coreward Rim and the Expansion Region for the first few weeks after the Revelations.

But those brushfires hadn't lasted long, and Guard HQ was soon able to turn its eye solidly toward the Edge, where a faction on Phoenix had already declared independence from the Council, and folks on Panamar were making real noise about doing so as well.

Xin had no idea how it was going on Phoenix, but if it was anything like Panamar, the answer was not well. Because even though the rebels on Panamar had technically outnumbered the Guard sent from the Core to put down the rebellion, and even though they were almost as well-armed as the Guard regs, they had absolutely no chance against the mechs.

The unofficial motto of the Guard 4th Light Mechanized Division was 'Death-On-Demand', and they delivered against that motto in devastatingly effective fashion. Xin hadn't been there for the first couple weeks of the conflict, but he had heard the stories. The rebels, confident in their numbers and itching for a fight, had actually set up blockades in the southern part of San Sebastian and had waited there for the Guard to come to them.

And the Guard came, though not in the manner they'd expected. After two weeks of largely futile attacks by local and still loyal Guard regulars, and even GPF regulars from the Core, one of the rebel soldiers had described feeling the mechs coming long before anyone had even seen them. Two tons of armored titanium steel alloy marching in a row two hundred strong shook the very planet itself under the rebels, and by the time the mechs had finally arrived and begun blasting the blockades, a good half the rebel soldiers had already fled in terror.

That brought two weeks of rebel victories to a hard stop, and what followed had been a desperate rearguard action by a group of the more professional rebel soldiers, most of them ex-Guard regs who had at least known that mechs landing on Panamar was a possibility. But even they had thought it unlikely. The Guard, after all, only had two light mechanized divisions for the entirety of the 47 Colonies, and they were both assigned to the Core.

Sending the mechs all the way to Panamar, therefore, had been an obvious message to anyone in the colonies thinking about following the insignificant planet's example: we will come at you with everything we have.

Now, four and a half weeks in, the Guard was clearly winning, and the rebels were losing more soldiers every day. Xin hadn't seen the official numbers, but rumor had it that a full 25 percent of the rebel forces had already been incapacitated or killed. And of the nearly one thousand mechs sent to Panamar to quash the rebellion, the rebels had only counted a dozen confirmed kills.

The overall rebel commander on Panamar was General Juan Bolivar, a short, compact, mustachioed man of forty-five years, who had been the commander of Panamar's only Guard Special Tactics unit just a few weeks before. Typically, GST commanders had to be enacters, but since enacters were so few on Panamar, the local Guard commissioner had made an exception. What the commissioner hadn't known was that Bolivar had been a rebel sympathizer since his earliest days on the planet, and he used his five years as GST commander to surreptitiously funnel weapons and supplies, which on paper showed as still sitting in Guard supply depots, to the rebellion. It was in large part because of Juan Bolivar that there even was a rebellion on Panamar, and he had been the natural choice to lead the fighting once the rebels came out in the open to challenge the Council.

That had made Xin automatically respect Bolivar when he'd arrived on planet. But the General had disabused him of that positive outlook quickly. The man may have been a rebel through and through, as well as a tactical genius, but he was also one of the most stubborn and infuriating men that Xin Wang had ever met. Xin had been sent to Panamar for the express purpose of serving as an observer and liaison for Admiral Gerald Williams, the overall leader of the rebellion's military, and Bolivar's effective superior. That alone should have afforded Xin at least some small status in the rebel camp.

But when he had arrived, Bolivar had refused to even see him or speak with him for three full days. And when he had finally summoned the pilot to his command tent, it was only to tell him that he was confiscating the shuttle he'd arrived in to help move troops from other parts of the planet to San Sebastian. Otherwise, he had steadfastly refused to listen to a thing Xin said or even recognize that he was part of Admiral Williams' staff. Xin had the sneaking suspicion that Juan Bolivar considered himself superior to the admiral as well but that he would never come out and say it because it would upset some of his troops who had heard rumors of the indomitable 'Admiral Ironsides' and held him up almost as a god or a talisman in their esteem.

Worse, tactical genius he may be, Bolivar was quickly demonstrating that he was at a severe disadvantage in his strategic thinking. And the rebels were losing badly under his command.

So now, Xin was literally stuck on Panamar, without his shuttle, and he couldn't even do the job he'd been sent to do. Instead, he was watching the dream of the rebellion die around him. But at the beginning of his third week on the planet and the fifth week of the Guard offensive against the rebels, Xin Wang finally got a break.

A small unit of rebels who had been separated from the main force a full week before in the city's southern sector had finally made contact. They had fled before a platoon of mech drivers who had pushed them out of the city into the jungles on the eastern edge. To return to the rebel camps, which were all in the western jungle, they'd had to circumnavigate the entire city on foot, avoiding Guard patrols and aerial drones as they went.

But in making their way out of the city, they had picked up a rather unusual prisoner.

Xin Wang had been flying with Dagger Squadron, of which he was still a titular member, when he had come to the rescue of a single fighter that had defended Gerald Williams' ship, the *Lucille*, from an attack by the Jaguari Pirates. Aboard that ship had been the first enacter in recorded history to defy the Council and his genetic programming, Tyrus Tyne.

Now, as he parted the flap on the small tent and let his eyes adjust to the darkened interior, he met another: Guard Private Feng Chu Hua.

When Xin first saw Feng Chu Hua, she was asleep in her small tent, two guards outside to keep her from escaping. The commander of the small rebel detachment that had found her had explained to Xin that the diminutive former mech driver had spent most of her time sedated. Even now, a full week from the time she claimed to have disobeyed her orders and deserted her Guard unit, the pain was strong enough that she had to be kept on constant painkillers and spent much of her time asleep.

It was so different than the story of Tyrus Tyne, who had reportedly only required a day or two to shed most of the pain of his own disobedience when he'd refused to follow his orders and kill Jinny Ambrosa. Xin wondered why the experiences were so different. But then again, he reflected, it was hard to draw any real conclusions from a sample size of two.

She'd awakened an hour or so after her arrival in the main rebel camp and, wincing in pain, had repeated her story to him, including the reasons for her desertion. And as she spoke, Lieutenant Commander Xin Wang started to form a plan that just might, if he was terribly lucky, turn the tide of the battle on Panamar.

FIFTEEN
FRIENDLY FIRE
PRIVATE TREVOR BENTLEY, GPF

Trevor Bentley hadn't joined the Guard because he'd wanted to be a symbol or paladin of peace and order. No, he joined because the judge had offered an entrance to the Guard Academy on Andromeda or five years in prison for grand theft auto.

Trevor shouldn't even have gotten that deal, but he'd scored high on one of the many standardized tests the Council doled out in high school, making the government believe he was somewhat of a genius. That he'd turned that genius into a successful career stealing 'unstealable' hovercars from rich neighborhoods didn't seem to dissuade the government from wanting to procure his services.

So, now he was here, on this Council-forsaken jungle hell under the light of a star that reminded him of a crimson red Altain Comet he'd once stolen from a banker who hadn't needed it (the man had four other high-end luxury cars, after all). And since he wasn't an enacter, he was fighting a group of heavily armed rebels wearing nothing but the body armor the Guard purchased from the lowest bidder, and that couldn't even stop some of the higher caliber anti-personnel rounds that the rebels seemed to have in abundance.

Trevor had almost died four times already, by his own count, since stepping foot on Panamar just three weeks before. The first had been when he was walking between barracks and almost stepped on a venomous snake—the planet was lousy with them. The second had been when a rebel group ambushed his squad in the southern part of San Sebastian, and only quick intervention by a mech squad had been able to save them from their pinned-down position.

That should have made Trevor like the mech drivers, but one of them, a lout named Hurley, had made far too big of a deal of 'saving the softies' and only added to the fuel of Trevor's anger.

The third near-death experience had been when an apartment building, declared safe by the mechs, had almost collapsed on top of him when he'd been inside with his squad checking for armed resistance.

And the fourth time had been in a side street when a rebel actually got off a shot that hit Trevor square in the chest. His body armor had stopped the round, but it had left a massive bruise on his chest that still hurt a week later.

Trevor had very quickly gone from a grunt content to put in his mandatory service time and then retire to somewhere he hadn't yet been busted for stealing cars to a terrified soldier who was absolutely certain he was going to die on this red-tinged hell of a planet.

Now, as he trudged down a random street in the middle of San Sebastian, he was sure his number was up. In the chaos of the battle, where split-second decisions often couldn't wait for the software integrated into Guard helmets and mechs to make up its mind about friends or foes, it was only a matter of time until someone died by friendly fire, and all the mechs stomping around scared him to no end. In fact, he was convinced it had to have already happened but that the Guard officers—a bunch of spineless desk jockeys, in his opinion—had probably covered it up.

And then it happened to his unit.

Trevor decided to take a shortcut and turned down an already-cleared alleyway between two apartment buildings with Corporal Tig. Tig was a young kid from Najeriya, two years younger than Trevor. Trevor hated most officers and noncoms alike, but Tig was the closest one to being OK in his book. The kid had never once hassled him for any of his common but minor infractions. And Trevor had grown to think of him as a sort of younger brother; he even had plans to see if he could convince Tig to join a highly illegal poker game held most nights in the barracks.

But Tig would never get a chance to win or lose any money in that game.

The mech driver would later claim that his IFF had tagged Tig and Trevor as enemy combatants. But the massive machine had rounded the corner so quickly that the two regs hadn't even had time to react before the spooked mech driver, not expecting to see anyone there, opened fire.

Tig had literally been dead before his body hit the ground, riddled by bullets from the two-ton mech's hand cannon. Trevor would have been next, but the mech's IFF miraculously tagged Trevor as a friendly just in time to lock up its gun even as the driver turned his way and reflexively kept pulling the trigger.

Now Trevor looked down at his dead friend and back up at the faceless mech. *This isn't over,* he thought with a cold certainty. *Someone's gonna pay.*

Trevor stood at attention—or rather, his approximation of attention, just stiff enough that he couldn't be reprimanded while still expressing his silent disdain for his commanding officer—in his captain's office in the barracks. He'd never even met the woman before. Captain Whats-Her-Name wasn't one to mingle with the troops, and besides, Trevor assumed the woman was just a worthless enacter lackey like most officers.

The woman in question was sitting at her desk with a nameplate that read Portenoy, largely ignoring Trevor's presence, letting the private stand at attention for longer than typically expected, no doubt as some sort of power play. Trevor was idly wondering if the woman had ever woken up with a snake in her bunk—anything to take his mind off of seeing Tig shot right in front of him—when the captain finally looked up and cleared her throat.

"At ease, Private."

Trevor waited a tick and then assumed a lazy stance that was much too casual for any situation in the presence of an officer; maybe he wanted to be reprimanded after the events of the day. But the captain said nothing, just frowned at her subordinate's obvious disrespect. *Probably doesn't want to deal with the paperwork a reprimand would generate,* Trevor thought.

"You went through something today that no soldier should ever have to go through, and you have my sympathies." To Trevor's ear, the woman didn't sound all that sympathetic. "But we need to ensure that this unfortunate incident doesn't affect morale in the division, don't you agree?"

Trevor said nothing in reply, and the captain's frown deepened. "I'm ordering you to tell no one what happened out there. Corporal Tig will be listed as killed in action so his family can know he died a hero. And as far as you and the rest of your platoon are concerned, that's exactly what happened. Are we clear?"

Trevor waited a moment, a dozen less-than-savory responses flashing through his head. But he simply shrugged and responded, "Clear, ma'am."

"Excellent. Dismissed Private."

As he left the woman's small office in the temporary barracks, and the captain could no longer see him, Trevor bared his teeth in anger. *Cursed mech jockeys are gonna pay.*

SIXTEEN
MECH DOWN
LIEUTENANT JOSE SANDOVAL, GPF

Jose Sandoval's war was going very poorly indeed. After he'd been the first Guard commander in history to 'lose' two of his enacters to supposed acts of disobedience, the senior commanders in charge of the policing action on Panamar had decided that he was just a little too inconvenient to have around. But unfortunately, the general had run out of mundane errands to inflict upon Jose.

Right before mess that same evening, his immediate superior, Captain Martindale, had taken Jose aside for a little chat. Jillian Martindale had graduated from the Guard command school four years ahead of Jose and had always treated the men and women underneath her reasonably well. That she hadn't been able to meet his eyes during their meeting was the first portent of doom.

"Lieutenant," she'd said—her refusal to use his first name as she usually did when speaking with her subordinate officers had been the second sign that this wouldn't be a conversation Jose would enjoy, "It has been decided that you are in need of more direct command experience."

In the end, Sandoval's sentence for his sins was to accompany his troops into the field for night operations. And now, here he was, one of the only Guard officers to actually participate in the battle, while his colleagues either slept warm in their bunks or watched from their command posts and communicated with their squads and non-coms via satellite uplink like Guard officers were supposed to do. Instead, Jose had eaten a hasty dinner and then jammed his body into a skinsuit that barely fit over his growing belly and then further jammed himself inside a command mech.

The command mechs had minimal weaponry: only a relatively small rail gun slung under the right arm. Instead, the computer power and space of the command mech were reserved for a sophisticated and powerful surveillance and comm suite, which allowed Sandoval to better control the battle around him, ordering his men and women around from among them rather than from his cushioned chair back at the base.

That the command mech he was using only had a few dozen hours on it when he'd first started driving it was testament to how seldom such mechs were actually employed. After all, why lead from the front when you had almost equal situational awareness and full contact with your platoon from the command center? The answer to that was simple: you led from the front when you'd done something to upset a commanding general.

He was plodding along in the rear of one of his squads, feeling sorry for himself, when the mech in front of him, driven by Corporal Hurley Ng of 1st Squad, suddenly collapsed.

Jose stopped walking, his mech grinding to a halt. "What's going on, Smoot?" he asked 1st Squad's sergeant while he tried to put his face through the proper sequence of expressions to command his HUD to magnify his view of Ng's fallen mech and stay switched on for night vision.

"Dunno, sir," Smoot's thick Dixie accent replied. "He said he was having some flickering in his HUD, and then he just stopped and collapsed."

"Well, I can see that!" Jose snapped a little more sharply than he'd intended. "But what caused him to collapse, and is he OK?"

"Checkin' now, sir," Smoot replied.

Sandoval waited impatiently and finally grew tired of just standing there and started walking slowly toward 1st Squad's position again.

"He's alive, sir," Smoot said once Sandoval had closed within five meters. "But he has no comms and his mech...it's frozen. Least, that's what I think he's tryin' ta tell us."

"How are you communicating with him if his comms are down?" demanded Jose.

"Uh, he's using head gestures. We can see him through his dome just fine... uh, sir." Smoot tried but failed to hide his consternation at having to explain something so simple to his lieutenant, but Jose was too upset by the situation to care.

"Any ideas as to what could have caused it?" he asked the man again with exaggerated patience.

"No, sir. We'll hafta get him outa the thing so we can talk to him. Probably do a diagnostic." The sergeant's accent tended to disappear when he used bigger official words like 'diagnostic', and it almost always amused Sandoval, but not today.

Jose looked back up and around at the burned-out city surrounding them. It looked deserted, but he knew that civilians scurried around them like rats through the rubble. Rebels mixed in with them, making it dangerous for the mech squad, even as heavily armored as it was, to stay in one place for too long. Many of the rebels had nothing more than small arms. But there was that AM launcher. The mere thought brought a stab of pain to Sandoval's head.

"Get him out of there, and let's hoof it back to base. We'll drag the mech."

Smoot raised both arms of his mech together and forward in the mech drivers' analog for a nod and started issuing orders to his squad. All the while, Sandoval nervously watched the buildings around them for heat signatures or other signs of the enemy. *I really hate it out here*, he thought for the hundredth time just that day, but the thought now carried an undercurrent of deeper worry. Mechs almost never broke down, and the sudden loss of Ng's comms, a system shielded from the rest of the mech's electronics so that it was usually the last thing to break, was even more concerning.

Something isn't right, he thought grimly and then started distracting himself by issuing orders to the other two squads under his command.

SEVENTEEN
BRICK WALL
LT. COMMANDER XIN WANG, FCN

General Juan Bolivar's biggest strategic mistake, to Xin's mind, had been even trying to engage the mechs. True, he'd given some of his forces heavier weapons, even a few AM launchers he'd managed to somehow pilfer from the GST weapons depot before the outbreak of hostilities. But the unfortunate thing about urban warfare was that the heavier weapons—an AM launcher could level a couple of city blocks—were just about useless unless you were willing to sanction high civilian casualties, which the rebellion wasn't. Not even Bolivar was that bloody, but he had steadfastly failed to see that giving his people weapons they wouldn't use against a foe they couldn't otherwise beat was just a recipe for slaughter.

It would have been better, Xin thought, to surrender the city and make the Guard come after the rebels in the jungles. The Guard had quickly stopped sending mechs along with their jungle patrols, as the thick undergrowth and close-together tree trunks made it next to impossible for the bulky machines to move at even a slow walking pace. If the rebels could draw the Guard into a jungle warfare campaign, it would negate the Guard's advantage and put the rebels back in the driver's seat, with their better knowledge of the jungles and their greater experience navigating and fighting in them. It would also draw the fighting away from heavily populated San Sebastian and reduce the chances of civilians being caught in the middle.

There had been little in the way of wars in the 47 Colonies, except for the occasional anti-pirate action or insurrection that the Guard put down. But Xin fancied himself a student of military history, and he had gotten his hands on some illegal history texts of Old Earth vintage. One of them talked about a war in a place called Vietnam, where a relatively small and lightly armed guerrilla force used a similar jungle to negate the advantages of an otherwise superior and better-equipped force, ultimately causing that superior force to get mired down and lose several key battles and the war.

Xin would have happily suggested the same to Bolivar if he could ever get a true audience with the man.

To Bolivar's credit, Xin had to grudgingly admit the man was stuck between a rock and a hard place. So far, the Guard mech units, and on fewer occasions the regs, had shown that they were willing to inflict wanton civilian casualties to draw out the rebels. Therefore, the man surely felt he had to keep sending rebels into the city to keep the civilians safe. The problem with that approach was that, against the mechs, the rebels were pretty much ineffective at stopping them from doing anything. Sure, they could slow them down a bit, but in the end, all they really accomplished was to add their own casualties to the growing number of civilians injured or killed.

The real problem that Lieutenant Commander Xin Wang had with General Juan Bolivar wasn't actually his decision to make that tradeoff, but rather the man's staunch refusal to admit that the tradeoff even existed. Bolivar took the approach of engaging the enemy whenever he could, whether it was in the best interest of the rebels—or the civilian population—or not. Indeed, he never seemed to question whether or not he should meet the enemy but almost seemed to consider it his moral duty to do so at all times. It made for some inspirational speeches to his troops but was lousy as a strategy for fighting an asymmetrical war.

The sad truth was that Xin knew that Juan Bolivar was in over his head. Admiral Williams had intimated that such might be the case when he'd sent Xin to Panamar to be his personal emissary on the ground. But as a mere lieutenant commander, the rough equivalent of a captain in Bolivar's army, Xin lacked the authority to do much more than watch. And he'd even been denied a front-row seat in doing that, finding himself instead effectively confined to the rebel command camp.

But today, he was going to *make* General Bolivar listen to him. He had a specific reason for that: Guard Private Feng Chu Hua. He had left her under a light guard in her tent for the time being and had gone to see Bolivar to argue for a new move in the war.

"She's an enacter who disobeyed, General," he found himself pleading with the man after he had argued loudly and invoked Gerald Williams' name several times just to get past the various staffers to see the general. "Imagine what that could do to Guard morale if it got out widely?"

"If she even is who she claims to be," the gruff Bolivar protested, studying the rudimentary holo map of San Sebastian in front of him and not even meeting Xin's gaze. "We have no proof; this could all be a ruse."

"To what end, General?" Xin had already tried several arguments with the older man, all of them rebuffed though without the general providing a single shred of evidence against them. "She doesn't have any intel to offer on troop movements in San Sebastian; it's been a week since she deserted. So if the Guard had her pretend to desert only to feed us false intel, there's just no point anymore. But she wears the uniform of a mech driver and knows all about how they operate; they only let enacters even get close to those things.

"Besides, we would pre-record the message and let you have final say on the contents before we send it out. That way, there's no way she could use it to pass intel on us back to the Guard. But honestly, General, I think she's sincere."

The argument Xin had been attempting to make for the last ten minutes with Bolivar was to let Feng Chu Hua tell her story in a message that they would broadcast planet-wide. His thought was that doing so might, at worst, breed distrust between the Guard regulars and enacters—convincing them that an enacter could disobey orders would create a wildcard between the two groups, which didn't get along well in the first place—and at best convince some of the Guard regulars that they were being lied to and used. The part of Feng's story about her late sergeant being ordered to endanger an infant would help there.

But Xin's biggest argument was that it was something new to try and couldn't possibly make things any worse, so why not try it? Bolivar disagreed, though he refused to give any concrete reasons why. For about the hundredth time since coming to the jungle hell of a planet, Xin silently berated Williams for sending him here on a doomed mission; it was made even worse because he couldn't even get a message out to Williams past the Guard fleet's blockade of the planet.

"Lieutenant," Bolivar often forgot to include the 'commander' part of his title, "I'll say this one more time. There's no way I'm letting that so-called enacter get on the air. So, if you're through wasting my time, I have a war to run!"

The man's snappish tone was enough to convince Xin that stubbornly staying and arguing would yield no fruit. With a half-hearted salute to the General, he left the command tent and stood outside for a long moment, looking up through the dense canopy at what little of the night sky showed through.

"Out of curiosity, what exactly would you have your deserter transmit?"

The question caught Xin off guard, and he looked around quickly and spotted the speaker, a tall man wearing fatigues, standing just a meter away and smoking a cigar. Xin would never understand that habit; smoking tobacco had been outlawed for centuries in the 47 Colonies, and he had never before known anyone who even wanted to break that particular law. But on Panamar, many of the citizens and rebels smoked regularly, as if to spite the government more than anything else. Still, the smell made Xin sick to his stomach every time.

"I beg your pardon?" he asked the stranger, buying himself time to think of the right answer or even figure out why the man was asking the question.

"You heard me," the stranger said with a smile. "You're just trying to decide if you should answer." He stepped closer to Xin and into a small patch of moonlight that had made its way through the trees to the jungle floor.

Xin was surprised that he did recognize the man, though he didn't know his name, but he was sure he was one of Bolivar's colonels who had been around the main command camp for the last few days.

"Colonel...?" he asked, studying the man in the dark.

"Kilgore," the man held out his hand, and Xin took it for a curt handshake. "Colonel Sam Kilgore, special operations group."

Xin raised an eyebrow, though he was sure the man couldn't see it in the darkness. "Special operations? I wasn't aware we had a group like that."

Kilgore shrugged and took another drag on the cigar, turning his head to blow out the smoke away from the pilot. "We don't. Not really. What I have is an under-strength battalion of about four hundred men and women who are just a bit better trained than the average soldier in our army. Mostly because we've all been fighting against the local Guard for the last eighteen years, ever since they tried to crack down on the tobacco trade here on the planet. Several folks took that poorly, and we've been fighting our own little guerrilla war ever since. We even win a battle here and there." Xin could see the man smiling around his cigar. "But you didn't answer my original question. What would you have that enacter traitor of yours broadcast if you had the chance?"

Xin thought carefully for a moment, worried that this might be some game Bolivar was playing, sending one of his underlings to find ways to discredit Williams' watchdog further. But he figured he didn't have any real credit to start with in the camp, so he shrugged and answered the man honestly.

"I'd have her tell her story: why she deserted and why her sergeant, who was also an enacter, killed herself rather than follow an immoral order."

"And just what do you expect that to accomplish?" the other man asked, but his tone was one of genuine curiosity, not challenge.

Xin let out a long breath and shook his head. "I'm hoping that someone over there might be as on edge as we are, honestly. That just maybe we might cause some internal rifts in the Guard ranks. I have to believe that there are some good men and woman over there, even among the enacters, who don't believe in their commanders' scorched earth policies, and that if they know there's an alternative, they might be willing to resist."

Kilgore shook his head. "Won't matter," he said, the cigar in his mouth only slightly distorting his voice. "Assuming your prisoner is telling the truth, that's still only three enacters in the history of the colonies that we know disobeyed the Council's orders. Even if you convinced a wildly optimistic one or two percent of the enacters over there to disobey, would that really change things?"

Xin felt his shoulders slump. "No, probably not," he admitted, shaking his head in frustration.

"But," the colonel continued as if he hadn't even heard the pilot answer, "if we could find a way to convince the non-enacters over there that they can't trust the enacters among them... Well, then maybe you'd have something."

Xin thought about this for a long moment, turning the idea over in his head and looking at it from a few different angles. He had made the same argument to Bolivar, but more out of desperation than actual belief it might work. "I suppose that makes sense," he finally responded. "But do you have any ideas on how to do it?" Then he shook his head emphatically. "Not that it matters. General Bolivar isn't willing to let me broadcast anything."

Kilgore reached up and removed the cigar from his mouth, then rubbed the back of the same hand on his beard stubble like he was scratching an itch. "I'm sure you could come up with some message that might accomplish the goal. I might have some ideas on that as well. But as for Bolivar not letting you, it's not even that he doesn't want to; he just can't."

"What do you mean?" Xin asked in surprise.

"We lost our last long-range transmitter capable of breaking through the Guard's jamming a few days ago, and the first thing that Guard fleet in orbit did was take out all of our satellites. Right now, we are blind and deaf; we don't even have contact with our men and women inside the city. There are low-powered radios for comms between teams and even between some of the closer camps, but anything more than a few kilometers is beyond us right now."

Xin shook his head rapidly to clear his mind and convey his shock. "You mean we keep sending troops into the city, and we don't even know what's happening to them?"

Kilgore shrugged and grimaced. "They send runners back to the various camps a few times a day to give Bolivar a general picture, but we have to be careful even with that; the Guard keeps trying to follow them and find the command camp. So, yeah, we're pretty much fighting this war blind."

"Thats... How?"

Kilgore shrugged again. "You ever hear the expression 'throwing good money after bad'? That's what we're doing at this point. We can't win. All we can do is try to keep fighting and make a statement. And who knows," he put the cigar back in his mouth and smiled around it, "your enacter friend might just help us make that statement a little louder."

Kilgore followed Xin back to Feng Chu Hua's tent, where they awoke the young woman from her pain-filled slumber to tell the colonel her story personally. And as she spoke, the gruff man started to nod, slowly at first, and then even smile a little toward the end.

EIGHTEEN
SABOTAGE
LIEUTENANT JOSE SANDOVAL, GPF

"What do you mean sabotage?!" hollered General Ostertag, a little bit of spittle flying from his mouth and hitting Jose Sandoval in the face. The lieutenant tried hard not to wince and further infuriate his commanding officer.

How do I keep ending up in this position? he thought with a healthy dose of self-pity. Until a few days ago, he'd never even been in the same room as the commanding officer of the 4th Light Mechanized Division. And now he was getting his second personal dressing down from the man in just the course of two weeks' time.

"Sir," he responded, putting as much calm respect into his voice as he could muster. "The techs found a virus in the mech's software package. Based on the timestamps, they say it was installed last night while the mech was undergoing recharge and general maintenance." He had already said all of this to the man once before, prompting the general's tirade, but now he tried to desperately reword the only information he had so that the general would stop shouting at him.

"Sabotage!" Ostertag exclaimed, slamming a fist on the holo table that took up the center of the command post. "Unless you're suggesting that one of the rebels got in here, that means it was one of the regs. Blasted softies."

"Sir?" Jose couldn't stop himself from asking.

The man speared him with a look that could melt iron and shook his head in exasperation. "Think Lieutenant. If it wasn't a rebel, and we'd know if any had infiltrated the base," Jose doubted if that were entirely true but wisely kept his thoughts to himself, "then it has to have been a member of the Guard. And everyone in my division is an enacter. So that leaves only the regs."

"Wasn't this Corporal Ng the one who shot that reg last week in that friendly fire incident?" The question came from one of the nameless myriad of staff officers who seemed to follow Ostertag wherever he went. The woman asking the question wore captain's bars on her uniform collar and reminded Jose of a woman he'd once gone on a date with who had stolen his wallet at the end of the night.

Ostertag frowned and reached up to rub his clean-shaven chin with one beefy hand. "That's right. I bet those blasted softies did this to get revenge, even though that whole incident was simply an honest accident."

The general looked over at another of his lackeys. "Get me General Nissen! Immediately!"

Jose felt a sinking feeling in his stomach but purposely kept his mind blank and refused to acknowledge the thought at the edge of his conscious mind. But he got a small headache anyway as the doubt and dismay crept in.

NINETEEN
REVENGE
PRIVATE JESSICA NEEL, GPF

"Blast!" Sergeant Sean Smoot threw his pad across the room. It bounced off the barracks wall and landed on one of the cots.

"Come on, Sarge, we can't prove it was the reg," soothed the calm voice of Private Jessica Neel.

"Wanna bet?! Who else but that Bentley kid could it have been?" Smoot whirled on his underling. "You saw the way that idiot softie has been skulking around the barracks. He has to be the one who sabotaged Ng's mech."

"So, what are we going to do, Sarge?" asked Private Harry Kraft from where he was lounging on his bunk.

Neel groaned internally. Smoot was just blowing off steam, but Kraft had a real mean streak. He was the squad troublemaker and had a reputation for bullying across the entire platoon; he may have been an enacter like the rest of them, but he excelled at finding nasty things to do that weren't specifically prohibited by orders. Lieutenant Sandoval, who was apathetic about the soldiers under his command, at best, even made it a habit to keep a closer eye on the belligerent young private.

"Keep out of it, Harry," she said, but the damage had been done. In Smoot's current state of mind, he needed little prodding.

"He's right, Jess," Smoot said, confirming her fears. "If Ostertag and Sandoval aren't going to do anything about this, we need to. That softie needs to know he can't mess with the Fourth!"

Jessica grimaced, not caring that the other two saw her. They were all enacters, and one of their standing orders prohibited intentionally killing any fellow guardmembers. So, Trevor Bentley was safe from that, at least. Apart from that, she'd been hoping that Sandoval or even Ostertag would order the platoon not to take any retaliatory measures. But they'd noticeably neglected to do that. She might have thought it was an intentional omission, but even heading down that train of thought gave her a good old enacter headache.

For a moment, she thought about leaving the room and warning someone, maybe even the softies, about what might happen. But Jessica Neel, as level-headed as she was, was no hero. And there were plenty of ways Smoot and Kraft could make her life miserable if she ratted them out.

TWENTY
COLLATERAL DAMAGE
CAPTAIN BOHDI PATEL, GPF

"Sir, we have a building full of civilians up ahead. Tac net shows some possible rebels in there, but there are a lot of women and children, too. What do you want us to do?"

Captain Bohdi Patel bit his lower lip and pulled up his tactical helmet's holo view to see what Lieutenant McAfee was talking about. The Tac Net indeed showed that the building currently housed three suspected rebels, but it only gave a 62% probability that the rebels were actually still in there; it was 38% likely that they'd already escaped through the maze of alleyways behind the large apartment building.

And the building was full of civilians, as McAfee had said. "Mac," he responded. "I say let's bypass the building, but leave a tac drone to watch for anyone exiting so we can circle back if we're wrong."

"Yes, sir. I—"

The lieutenant's reply was cutoff by a garble of static, and then a stern voice cut into the comm channel. "This is Major Garland of the 4th Mech, Charlie Company. We marked that building you're yapping about for demo two minutes ago. Why is it still standing?"

"Major, sir," Bohdi replied carefully, "we have a low probability that there are any rebels left in the building, but it is full of civilians: 67, read six seven, to be exact. I'm of the opinion that the collateral damage is too high to—"

"I don't care what your opinion is, *Captain*!" The man emphasized Bohdi's lower rank. "I'm ordering you to demo the building so that it doesn't present a threat to my company's rear. Are you going to follow the order or not?"

Bohdi stood in shocked amazement, his mouth moving but no words coming out. He was grateful that the comm channel was voice only so the major couldn't see his facial expression. Finally, he found the words. "I'm sorry, sir, but I cannot follow that order. I believe it conflicts with the Guard Articles of Paramilitary Operations, section five, paragraph six." That paragraph prohibited collateral damage of greater than five civilians in any action unless there was a clear and present danger to the Guard unit performing such action. This situation did not meet that criteria in Bohdi's mind—not even close.

"Oh, yeah?" the major challenged belligerently over the comm. "Well I have different standing orders. So, you have thirty seconds to clear your men from the vicinity of that building, or I won't be responsible for what happens to them."

"Wait, sir, are you saying you're going to—" Another burst of static interrupted Bohdi's protest, signaling that Major Garland had dropped from the comm channel.

"No, no, no, no," Bohdi found himself repeating. "Lewie, get your guys away from that building. I've gotta stop this!"

Not waiting for the Lieutenant's response, Bohdi started sprinting toward the location on the Tac Net that showed where Garland's Charlie Company was moving toward the doomed building. Garland himself wasn't among them, of course. Mech officers usually rode out battles from behind a desk in the command center, but his helmet holo helpfully highlighted the senior non-com in the group of mechs, and Bohdi ran toward the man's location with everything he had.

As he ran, he unsuccessfully tried to open a comm channel to the man, a Staff Sergeant Govind Porter, but he wasn't responding. *He's probably on with Garland right now,* Bohdi thought in desperation and tried to pour more speed into his sprint.

He rounded the corner a block away from Porter's location at

Garland's threatened 30-second mark and saw a row of mechs holding up their left arm launchers and smoke trails streaking toward the large apartment building. In horror, he watched the building tremble with the explosions of more than a dozen well-placed rockets at critical structural points. As the building crumbled in on itself, Captain Bohdi Patel stopped and fell to his knees. He heard shouts of despair as if the doomed denizens of the building were crying out in one last exclamation of shock and terror. But he quickly realized that the voice crying out was his own.

TWENTY-ONE
PLAN OF ATTACK
EX-PRIVATE FENG CHU HUA, GPF DESERTER

A week before, Feng Chu Hua had been as faithful and obedient as any enacter in the 4th Mechanized. Now, she was plotting an attack against her old unit. This brought two kinds of pain to her. First was the pain her subconscious continued to levy on her for disobeying orders. That pain had, luckily, faded a bit each day, but it was still rather severe, especially at night, and she shuddered to think of what it would be like without the constant diet of painkillers the rebel medics had her on.

The second pain, however, was worse. She was a traitor, and not just to her division and the officers who had ordered Sarah Nowak to kill an infant and were ordering similar atrocities all over San Sebastian, but also to her friends. Her face kept going to Corporal Harrison Walker. If Sergeant Sarah Nowak had been like an older sister to her, Walker had been like an only-slightly-older brother. She felt equal parts in awe of him and protective of him, and what she was doing now might very well result in his death. The feeling was enough to make her want to crawl back to her tent and sleep away both sets of pain.

She looked over at Xin Wang. The earnest young pilot had been the first rebel soldier to believe her story without reservation and, for the last four nights, had held her hand and dabbed her burning forehead when the agony had made its nightly resurgences. She had very quickly learned to trust him, not just to help her but also to do what was right for the people of Panamar. She had to believe that he was going to use her information in the right way, even if that meant some of her friends might die. But even the thought of saving a thousand infants like the one Sarah had died to protect didn't make her feel one iota better about the possibility of Harrison Walker dying.

"We enter the camp on the south end, opposite the city. It should be the most lightly guarded and the last direction they expect trouble from." Colonel Kilgore motioned in the holo map to show the exact area he was referring to. "Then we split into two groups: one takes out the jammers; the other hits the comm shack and broadcasts Ms. Feng's message. We move in hard and fast and make sure that by the time they scramble to the alarms, we're in the comm center."

He stepped back, looking at the assembled rebels in the room. Most of them were intently studying the holo and nodding along. All of them were frowning.

"It won't work." Xin Wang's voice was calm but authoritative and said what Feng herself had thought the instant she heard Kilgore's broad outline of a plan. For not the first time, Chu Hua wondered at how such a young man as Xin could have such a high level of confidence, especially when, as far as she could tell, he was little more than a semi-welcome interloper in the rebel camp.

Kilgore arched an eyebrow and motioned for the short pilot to continue.

"You're thinking two-dimensionally," Xin said, waving toward the holo image. "And because of that, you're playing right into the Guard's hands; they only have to protect against a fixed set of ingress points, and they know those points better than we do.

"Well, better than most of us." He nodded toward Feng, who stood on his right. "What's worse, they have the mechs. Per Feng's intel, only two or three of those are patrolling the camp at any given time, but the second we go in, we have to assume those mech drivers will be rushing to their machines."

"But her intel also tells us they take a while to get those things moving from a cold start, up to fifteen minutes. It's plenty of time," argued one of the younger men in the tent, a Captain whom Feng hadn't seen before.

Xin shook his head. "So, all that means is that they won't be ready for us going in, but unless everything goes perfectly, they will be ready when we're on the way out if we hit even the slightest delay. And we don't even know what kind of access controls will be in that comm center; Feng's never even been in there."

"All of that's a problem," Kilgore admitted. "But we are on a planet's surface; this isn't a space battle, so it's naturally going to be a two-dimensional plan. We can't exactly come from below; we don't have any tunneling equipment, and the soil in this area is too light and loamy to allow for a stable tunnel anyway, even if it wouldn't take us weeks to build one. And we can't come from above; the Guard owns the airspace, unless we want to put our few lightly armed shuttles against those dropships and air superiority fighters, and that's assuming that fleet in orbit doesn't launch their own fighters the second the alarm sounds." He stopped, looking at Xin expectantly, his tone and mannerisms not those of someone on the defensive but genuinely interested in what the young man would say in return.

"Hold on," Xin replied and stepped up to the table. Sticking both hands into the holo field, he grabbed the image of the Guard HQ camp and spun his hands, rotating the entire image so that it was now perpendicular to the surface of the holo table like he'd somehow ripped the camp out of the ground and turned it on its edge.

"Look at it from this angle," he said. "You're right about the tunneling. It wouldn't work. And you're right about the airspace." He gestured a few more times. A red latticework appeared over the camp, or rather, to the side of the rotated image of the camp, symbolizing the Guard's control of the skies. He stepped back so all could see.

Kilgore had been rubbing the stubble on his chin, his expression one of curiosity, but now his eyes went wide, and he smiled. "There's a gap," he said softly.

Now Feng saw it, too. In the air between the top of the camp—now its side—and the Guard-controlled airspace was a gap of twenty centimeters that, in the real-world scale the image represented, would be about 100 meters.

"If this were a target space station and I was piloting an attacking fighter," Xin continued, "I would fly into this gap here, and then I would turn my fighter laterally and let inertia carry me forward, strafing the 'camp' as I go. If I'm moving fast enough, I'm too close for the station's—the camp's—weapons to target me with any degree of accuracy. And even if the enemy controls this entire area..." He waved at the red latticework of the Guard-controlled airspace.

"They can't fire on you because they'd hit their own station," Kilgore finished for him, a smile gracing his typically stern features. "But that's in a space battle. How do we make a strafing pass like that, meters above a planet's surface? We would never get our shuttles close enough to their camp without them seeing them and taking them out."

It was Xin's turn to smile. "Tell me, Colonel, have you ever been zip lining?"

Kilgore's smile got wider.

TWENTY-TWO
ESCALATION
CAPTAIN BOHDI PATEL, GPF

Major Tiffany Rodriguez frowned across her desk at her underling, Captain Bohdi Patel. "I'm not going to lie to you, Bohdi. You're in deep on this one. That Major Garland went all the way to Colonel Klipinger, and he just gave me an earful about you disobeying a direct order."

"Come on, Tiff," Bohdi said, leaning forward. "That order was patently illegal, and Garland knew it. I was under no obligation to obey it, no matter what his enacter superiors told him to do."

Rodriguez frowned. "Captain, it's 'Major' right now, understood?"

Bohdi frowned back but nodded. "Yes, Major."

"Now listen, I know you, Captain, and you're a good soldier, but you have got to get it through your head that not everything can be done by the book. And even a lot of those regulations are open for interpretation. In this case, you should have—"

"Major," he said, cutting her off. "Sorry, but this one wasn't even borderline. That guy killed 67 civilians, including women and children, to possibly get one or two rebels. Tell me how that's open to interpretation."

For a long moment, neither of them spoke. Bohdi looked Rodriguez dead in the eyes, challenging her to disagree, and she looked back hard at him. It was a battle of wills, but in the end, there could be no winners today.

"Look, Bohdi," she said, her voice softening. "I understand how you feel about this one, but Klipinger isn't happy. I went out on a limb and told him it wouldn't happen again, that you were just combat fatigued and made a bad call. Stopped him from busting you down to lieutenant, but just barely. As it is, he's still pretty upset, and I just used a big part of my political capital with the man to save your butt on this one."

Bohdi sat back and sighed. "I know, Tiff—Major—and I'm grateful. But sixty-seven people. When did we become the bad guys in this war?"

Rodriquez frowned but didn't argue with him...or agree with him. Neither she nor Bohdi were enacters, but that didn't make it prudent or safe to speak that openly against the Guard, and Bohdi knew it. When she spoke again, her voice had lost all of its earlier edge. "Get some sleep, Bohdi. You and I both know that this won't be the last time we have to do something that we don't agree with. At least if you're rested, you can choose your battles. There have to be good officers like you out there, or things will get even worse, you hear me?"

"Yeah, I hear you," he said grudgingly. He was actually surprised by how candid she'd risked being about it, and his level of respect for her went up another notch, along with another feeling toward her. He raised an eyebrow. "You know, there are other ways for a weary soldier to rest."

She smirked and huffed in response. "Right, and if Klipinger finds out we share more than a command, he'll bust us both down to private, won't he? The man is a decent senior officer, but he's an enacter through and through."

Bohdi tried to look like her words hurt, but he could tell she wasn't buying it. Then he decided to get serious again, for a moment. "Tiff, does it ever bother you that you've risen as high in the Guard as you can because you're not one of them?"

The 'them' in this case was obvious to both of them. Even reaching the rank of major was an almost incomprehensible feat for a non-enacter like Tiffany Rodriquez. And before today's incident, it looked like Bohdi himself was on the fast track to repeat that feat. Not bad for a kid originally enlisted to avoid a jail sentence, but he strongly doubted that was the case anymore.

"You know the drill," she said, a false lightness in her tone that didn't fool him for a second. "Ours is not to reason why..."

"Ours is but to do or die," he finished the bastardized quote for her. "I get it, but sometimes I just feel like we're all expected to be soulless robots, whether we're enacters or not." His voice rose, and he knew he should stop there, but something demanded he keep going. "And maybe that wasn't so bad when we were fighting pirates, but now we're fighting our own citizens, and a lot of innocent people are getting caught in the meat grinder!"

"Careful who you say that around!" she snapped back. It wasn't the first time they'd had the conversation, but every time, they risked much simply by voicing their concerns. "Now, why don't you get some chow while the food is still lukewarm?"

He gave her a tired and frustrated smile and stood from the chair, saluting her sloppily, before he turned and took a short step to open the door of the tiny office.

"And Captain," her voice followed him.

"Yes, Major?"

"I've changed my mind. After you eat, come and see me for a more thorough debriefing."

Normally, an invitation to Tiff's quarters was a surefire way to put a smile on his face, but not this time. He would go, of course, but the memory of those 67 dead civilians wouldn't be banished quite that easily.

TWENTY-THREE
HEADACHE
LIEUTENANT JOSE SANDOVAL, GPF

"What's up, Corporal?" Jose Sandoval asked, looking up from his desk holo at Harrison Walker, who stood timidly in the doorway to his small office.

"Sorry to disturb you, sir. May I speak with you?"

Just over a week before, Jose's answer would have been to direct the young corporal back to his immediate superior, but that had been Sarah Nowak. So, he gave a small smile that he knew didn't reach his eyes and motioned for the young man to take a seat at the single guest chair across from his desk.

"What's on your mind, son?"

Walker looked down at his hands, clasped together in his lap as if trying to find in them the courage to say whatever it was he'd come to say. Finally, he looked up shyly and spoke his mind.

"Well, sir, it's just that I have a lot of questions with the Sarge gone and Feng missing. I know they ordered us not to speak about them, but I figured it was OK to do so inside the platoon since you and I already are in the know."

By the way the young man visibly winced, Sandoval could tell that his subconscious was punishing him for his liberal interpretation of orders, but he chose not to add to the man's pain by reprimanding him. He didn't stop to reflect on the fact that he would have strongly rebuked Walker for such a thing just days earlier—that thought would lead him down a rabbit hole he was doing his best to avoid.

"What are your questions, Corporal?" he asked gently, feeling a dull ache in his own head now.

Walker looked down at his feet and shuffled them a bit. "It's just, sir, that I know we're enacters and all, but... Well, sir, if the rumors about Nowak are true, what would you have done?"

Sandoval frowned. He hadn't been aware that there were rumors going around as to what had really happened with Nowak. Maybe some of the regs had seen it happen, or someone in the division had blabbed before the orders had been handed down to avoid speaking of the incident. Either way, it wasn't good.

Worse, Sandoval had no idea how to answer the question. Even thinking about it made his headache pound harder. Besides, he had been the one who had given Sarah Nowak the order. At first, he had been indignant, angry even, that she'd disobeyed it and gotten him into so much trouble. But for the last week and a half, that feeling had been slowly replaced by a strange and foreign sense of guilt.

Guilt around orders was something they drilled out of you in the Enacter Academy. It was illogical, they taught, to feel guilt over something that you had no choice but to do. And it was disloyal, they taught even more, to feel guilt over something the Council asked you to do, because the Council was always good, and just, and right.

Jose had believed that then. He was less sure now. And seeing what Sarah did and having to face the reality that maybe there was another choice... Well, it was all playing havoc on his sense of how the galaxy worked.

Still, he couldn't say that out loud to Walker, could he?

"Corporal, the beautiful thing about being an enacter is that you don't have to worry about the morality or even legality of your orders. First of all, trust that the Council and its duly appointed leaders have more information than you do. What looks wrong to someone standing on the outside is undoubtedly right when looked at through the Council's greater knowledge. And anything the Council orders us to do is, by definition, legal.

"Second, you can't disobey your orders, so worrying about whether they're right or wrong is just a waste of mental power and a great way to bring some real pain down on yourself. Because when guardmembers disobey orders, people die.

"My suggestion is that you need to forget all about Sarah Nowak and Feng Chu Hua. Let's get you reassigned to another squad now that it's just you and Jennings in the Second. I think the isolation is putting you in the wrong head space. Sound good?"

"Uh, yeah, sure, Lieutenant. Thanks, I guess." The boy was clearly disappointed, but Sandoval knew that further discussion down the path Walker wanted to take would lead to nothing but pain for both of them. He gestured to the hall to show the boy he was dismissed and watched him leave slowly.

Strangely enough, Jose was surprised to find, in retrospect, that he'd given the young corporal the canned Academy answer to his question not because he himself believed that answer any longer but more to save the young man from feeling the same guilt and pain that Jose himself was now grappling with.

His headache had gotten a lot worse in the last few moments. But for the first time in a long time, he almost welcomed the pain and kept right on thinking.

TWENTY-FOUR
BRICK WALL REVISITED
LT. COMMANDER XIN WANG, FCN

"It's ludicrous! That's what it is. And no soldier under my command will take part in something so foolhardy!"

Xin resisted the urge to roll his eyes. General Juan Bolivar was at it again. Xin and Kilgore had asked for a private audience with the man, but he'd insisted instead on them presenting their plan in the middle of the command tent with a full audience. And now he seemed to be playing to the crowd.

"Sir, if you'll just let us—" started Kilgore, but Bolivar chopped a hand through the air to cut him off.

"Colonel, I'm disappointed in you. I would expect something like this from a half-cocked know-nothing fighter pilot." He jerked his head toward Xin. "But not from you. How did you let him talk you into this mess of a plan?"

"Sir, it was *my* plan," Kilgore said, his voice calmer than Bolivar's but containing an edge of anger nonetheless.

It hadn't strictly been Kilgore's plan. The truly crazy part had come from Xin, and then Kilgore had filled in the blanks. But both men had agreed that presenting it as the colonel's plan was less likely to automatically trigger the general's wrath than anything presented to him as coming from the 'know-nothing fighter pilot'.

Now, it seemed they'd been wrong. Bolivar had lost contact with four full platoons that afternoon. With long-range comms jammed, no one could be sure what had happened to them, but the fact they'd all missed their planned rendezvous made it likely that they'd been killed or captured—most likely the former, given the way the Guard was operating in San Sebastian. On top of that, they had several reports of Guard units indiscriminately taking out civilians in the hopes of taking out rebels along with them. Most of the reports were unconfirmed, but there was a disturbing pattern emerging.

That had put the general in a foul mood, and he was taking it out on Kilgore and Xin now for lack of better targets. Never mind that it was the man's own incompetence—at least from Xin's point of view—that had led to him losing so many soldiers over the last few weeks. Bolivar certainly wasn't going to admit that, not even to himself, so his subordinates—and one 'know-nothing fighter pilot'—were obviously to blame for all of his troubles.

"Sir, if we could just—" Kilgore tried again. But as before, Bolivar wouldn't let him finish.

"Get out of my sight, Colonel. And confine this hopped-up space jockey to his quarters, along with that mech traitor. I don't want either of them meddling in my command again!"

With a finality that spoke volumes, the general turned his back on Kilgore and walked away and out of the tent.

For a moment, Xin thought he saw a fire in the colonel's eyes, but it faded too fast for him to be certain. Motioning for Xin to follow him, Kilgore left the tent through the opposite side.

"Of all the—" Xin started as soon as they were out of earshot.

"Not now," Kilgore calmly cut him off as he stopped to light a cigar and then tossed the spent match on the ground. "I'm escorting you to your tent, remember?" The way he said it left no room for argument, so Xin shut his mouth and followed along.

But when Kilgore stopped at a tent, it wasn't the small one that Xin called his quarters, but the larger one with the holo table where they'd formulated their plan. Xin opened his mouth to ask Kilgore what he was doing, but the man cut him off again with a look.

They entered the tent and found Feng Chu Hua pacing anxiously inside. "Well?" she asked, whirling to face them.

Kilgore just shook his head, and the diminutive woman's shoulders slumped.

"I'm to take you both to Lieutenant Wang's quarters and have you confined there," he told her simply. She opened her mouth to argue, much as Xin had, but he shook his head and then moved his eyes to indicate the tent door they'd entered through.

Picking up on the hint, Xin said loudly. "But Colonel, I'm a representative of Admiral Williams himself. General Bolivar has no legal authority to confine me or even issue me a command."

Kilgore half-smiled. "Since when does 'legal authority' mean anything in an illegal rebellion? General Bolivar is the commander on the ground, and you will be confined per his orders. Now, come along quietly, you two, and there won't be any trouble."

The stern tone coming from the colonel's mouth was in sharp contrast with the half-smile that same mouth still wore, and Feng stopped with her mouth open, looking back and forth between Kilgore and Xin with a confused expression.

Xin shook his head at her, and she shut her mouth. "I protest in the strongest terms possible," he said to Kilgore, but for now, Ms. Feng and I will retire to my quarters until we can sort out this mess."

"Very well, Lieutenant Commander. I will find someone to escort you shortly. Until then, you are not to leave this tent!"

Now Chu Hua opened her mouth again, but Kilgore held up a finger to his lips and motioned with the other hand again toward the tent door. In the silence that followed, they heard the sound of footsteps as someone outside tried—and failed—to quietly retreat from where they'd been listening outside the tent flap.

After a full minute passed and they heard nothing more, Kilgore shook his head ruefully. "Well, I wish I could say that was surprising."

"What, that Bolivar sent someone to spy on us?" Xin asked dryly. "You had to see that coming."

The other man shrugged. "I'd at least held out some hope that he still trusted me, but apparently, he's further out of his mind than I thought." He shook his head sadly.

"Would someone please tell me what is going on?!" Feng practically shouted, though she pitched her voice in something approximating a whisper.

"The good general wouldn't even hear our entire plan. At the first mention of what we intended to do, he shot us down like a pregnant duck on solstice," Xin explained.

Both Feng and Kilgore gave him a confused look. "Sorry," he said. "It's an old saying on Manchuria. Basically, he wouldn't listen to any of the colonel's arguments and commanded him instead to confine the two of us to my quarters. But I'm assuming Colonel Kilgore has a way around that." He pitched the last sentence up a bit to turn it into a question.

Kilgore frowned. "Not much of one, I'm afraid. There aren't many people here who will go against the general, either from fear or misplaced respect. There are...grumblings around the camp that he's losing his touch. It would be surprising if there weren't after all the casualties we've suffered. But not enough that anyone would openly defy him.

"Still, he's obviously paranoid, or he wouldn't have sent one of his lackeys to spy on us and make sure I was following his orders. I used to be in his inner circle, but I've spoken up a few too many times against some of his decisions, and... Well, I think it's safe to say I am no longer in the man's good graces."

"There has to be something we can do," Chu Hua pleaded.

"Actually, I have an idea about that," Xin said, drawing a surprised look from both of his companions. He turned to Kilgore. "How is Bolivar sending orders to the other camps with the comms jammed?"

The tall man thought for a moment, then responded slowly. "His transmitters can still reach the close in camps, and some of them relay his messages to others. But for the further out camps, messengers. He sends them on a fixed schedule. Once early each morning to carry the tactical orders for the day, and once again every evening to get the day's report and carry the strategic plan, such as it is, for the next day. At least, that was what he laid out to us."

Xin nodded thoughtfully. "And those same messengers bring back news from the outlying camps, right?"

"Yes." Kilgore drew out the word, making it clear he didn't see where Xin was going with his line of questions.

"Would you happen to know the routes these messengers take? Say, between here and the special operations camp four klicks to the west? I'm assuming that one is far enough out to need a messenger?"

The colonel's eyes widened in surprise and understanding. "Why yes, just far enough. And I do know the route; it's the same one I use to get back and forth to my unit. It's a roundabout path to fool any spy satellites that might penetrate the jungle canopy and try to follow the messenger's heat signature. A bit silly because if they can't see us in these camps, then they certainly won't see a single messenger trudging through the jungle."

Xin remembered being briefed when he'd first arrived on Panamar just weeks before, when some of Bolivar's men had at least pretended to afford him the respect warranted for an emissary of the rebellion's supreme military commander, that the jungle canopy of the hellish world had high concentrations of certain metals, leached from the soil. That, combined with the ever-present humidity, made most satellite tracking completely ineffective. The metal blocked radar, the density of the canopy blocked visual sensors, and the heat and humidity combined with the thick jungle made thermal imaging next to worthless.

That had been one of the arguments for keeping the camps so small and spread out: first, because they could better stay under the jungle canopy that way, and second, because about the only chance the Guard had of finding the camps was to try to follow the rebel troops or stumble blindly through the jungle until they ran into them.

"So, if we know the route the messenger takes, say this evening, what if we were to intercept them and...relieve them of their burden?"

"That burden being the next day's general order of battle and any message Bolivar might send about you, Ms. Feng, and me being on his list of deplorables?" Kilgore asked with a gleam in his eye.

Xin shrugged. "You said it, not me. Can we make it work?"

Feng broke in before Kilgore could answer. "But what does that buy us?"

Kilgore smiled widely. "The lieutenant commander is far sneakier than I gave him credit for, even after helping us with such a genuinely sideways battle plan. You see, if we take the place of Bolivar's messenger, we can tell the outlying special operations camp anything we want. And if I arrive in place of the messenger, they will naturally assume I'm there to brief them on a special mission."

"That's right," Xin said. "And what better troops to storm the Guard HQ than a bunch of spec ops grunts?"

Chu Hua smiled in appreciation of the daring plan.

"Except for one thing," Kilgore said, his smile fading. "I won't do it, not like that."

"Wha—" Xin started to ask, his heart sinking. Chu Hua also looked distressed. But the man cut him off.

"I know those spec ops boys and girls each by name and a whole lot more; they've all been under my command for years, and the mission we'll be asking them to undertake is one that many of them won't come back from. I won't lie to them and tell them the orders come from the general."

"Then we've already lost," Xin said dejectedly.

But Kilgore's half-smile returned. "Not necessarily. My spec ops unit happens to be one of the least enamored with Bolivar right now. He's been using it like a band-aid to patch up his terrible battle plans—sending them where things fall apart because of his incompetence. I'm willing to bet that at least some of them will go along with the plan because it makes sense and maybe even because Bolivar is against it. And others will go along with it because they view me as their commander, not Bolivar."

"But what about the ones who don't?" Feng asked.

Kilgore shrugged. "As long as they don't actively try to stop us, we can be long gone with the willing troops before the unwilling ones can get word back to Bolivar. It's worth a shot."

Xin begrudgingly nodded. "It's the only shot we have. And I can't argue—even though I want to. I don't want their deaths on my conscience, either. But it is quite a risk."

"So is being a rebel," Kilgore said grimly. "And a traitor." He nodded toward Feng.

"I'm in. Let's do it," Xin said resolutely.
Feng just nodded.

TWENTY-FIVE
BEATING
PRIVATE TREVOR BENTLEY, GPF

Trevor Bentley crouched in the darkness between two of the temporary barracks buildings. The light from his cigarette illuminated the plasticrete walls of the modular Guard buildings.

Smoking was illegal in the 47 Colonies. But just like any drug, there was always a way to get tobacco. This particular strain was a local one he'd helped himself to from an apartment building they'd cleared in San Sebastian. It tasted terrible, but stolen meant free, and it gave him a buzz from the nicotine and the rush of doing something illegal in the middle of a heavily patrolled Guard camp.

He took a long drag and blew out the smoke in something nearing ecstasy. But he was jerked abruptly from his relaxed state by the appearance of two shadows at the far end of the narrow alley. He didn't recognize either silhouette except that both were men and short. He turned and looked behind him and saw two more.

Dropping the cigarette, Trevor considered yelling, but the figures started moving toward him before he could decide what to do.

TWENTY-SIX
JUNGLE TREK

EX-PRIVATE FENG CHU HUA, GPF DESERTER

They had ambushed the messenger about halfway along his circuitous route between Bolivar's command camp and the special operations camp. The young man had obviously gotten a bit too comfortable with his back-and-forth duty well outside the zone of any fighting and hadn't even gotten his weapon drawn before Kilgore and Xin had pinned his arms and taken the gun away from him.

Feng Chu Hua watched this all happen, feeling both useless and helpless. She had been a good mech driver with the potential to be a great one. But outside of a few basic courses at the Guard Academy, she had little to no experience in hand-to-hand combat. Not that a woman who weighed barely 45 kilograms soaking wet would be much of a threat to the average male soldier—unless she fought dirty, and she admitted to herself she definitely wasn't above taking a cheap shot to win a fight.

But for now, she was essentially an observer while Kilgore and Xin subdued the young messenger. Xin had suggested leaving the man tied to a tree, but the colonel had sharply objected. "In this jungle, he'd be dead in hours. There are a lot of things more dangerous than the Guard roaming these trails."

And that was that. They dragged the messenger with them the

remaining two kilometers to the camp. At first, the boy—who couldn't have been more than eighteen years old—fought them every step of the way. But then Kilgore had pulled him aside and said something to him in a low tone that Feng couldn't make out. The boy's eyes had gone wide, and he'd stopped resisting, following along after them like a particularly obedient puppy.

They kept a brisk pace, but the jungle slowed them down, so they arrived at the special ops camp about 30 minutes later. The sentry at the camp's edge saluted Kilgore sharply and threw only a short, confused glance at the messenger with his hands bound in front of him.

Two minutes later, they were in the command tent at the center of the camp, waiting while one of the soldiers went to fetch the camp commander.

They were joined shortly by a tall man with a strong jaw and a surprisingly open face. He smiled as he drew himself up in front of Kilgore and saluted, though he did it with a semi-lazy wave of the hand that surprised Feng.

"Colonel, it's good to have you back," the man said, asking no questions but raising an eyebrow at the odd entourage Kilgore had brought to the camp.

"Major Evans, this is Lieutenant Commander Xin Wang, emissary from Admiral Williams." The man's other eyebrow went up at that. "And this is former Guardswoman Private First-Class Feng Chu Hua of the 4th Light Mechanized Division."

Feng hadn't thought it possible, but the major's eyes went even wider.

"But the 4th Mech, they're all..."

"Enacters. Yes," Kilgore replied. "But I assure you that she truly is —somehow—a traitor. She gave us information on their forward operating base and barracks. Some of it I already had, but she couldn't have known that. She didn't lie or hide anything. So, I trust her."

Now, it was Chu Hua's turn to look surprised. She reminded herself not to underestimate the colonel.

"So," Evans said, turning to look Kilgore in the eyes. "I'm guessing by the tied-up messenger you left outside the tent that you're not here on official business."

Kilgore frowned and shook his head. "I'm sorry, Keith. Bolivar had me removed from command and had put these two under arrest. The losses are getting worse, and that's getting to him. The loss of comms only made it harder for him to get a handle on things, and he's lashing out.

"We're here because we have a plan to stop the comm jamming and to let our traitorous enacter friend here get her story out to the rest of the Guard."

Evans raised an eyebrow again. "Oh, is that all?" He turned and looked at Chu Hua. "And you think that getting your message out will, what, convince other enacters to disobey their orders too? I didn't even think that was possible?"

"What about the Revelations?" Xin broke in, giving Feng the time to put her answer together.

Evans half-smiled. "Listen, I appreciate the stories Siefred told as much as the next person, but I believe there was a healthy bit of propaganda mixed in with the facts. I mean, an alpha disobeying the Council's orders? Come on."

Chu Hua saw Xin's jaw clench and knew the major had hit a soft spot. "Listen, Major," he ground out. "I met Tyrus Tyne. Well, he was asleep at the time, but I met Reader Jinny Ambrosa, who was with him. And Admiral Williams believes the stories; he met Tyne before and after his...incident—saw him when he was an obedient enacter and later a traitor to the Council."

Evans gave Xin an appraising look. "I apologize, Lieutenant Commander. And I stand corrected." He turned and regarded Feng again. "But my question remains. Do you think that sharing your story is going to convince other enacters to follow your lead?"

Despite her best efforts, she felt hot tears start to fill her eyes. "I-I, uh, I wasn't the first. Here on Panamar, I mean. My sergeant—my friend—she disobeyed first. Something about her, doing what she did, it changed me. Maybe it will change others."

Evans said nothing about the tears but gave her a sympathetic smile. "Losing a comrade in arms can do that."

Xin jumped back in. "Honestly, we don't know if it will change anything for the enacters, but we're hoping we can at least drive a wedge between the Guard enacters and the regs."

"Well," Evans turned to Kilgore. "Obviously, I'm in. What do you want to tell the men?"

"The truth," the colonel answered. "They deserve that. It will be a strictly volunteer mission."

Evans smiled. "OK, let's hear your plan then."

An hour later, after Kilgore and Xin had taken Evans through the plan in detail, answering his pointed questions and addressing his doubts. Along the way, he offered several suggestions that strengthened it as well.

Evans sat back in his chair at the small table they'd gathered around. "It's audacious, I'll give you that. And with a few more tweaks, it just might work. But I'm thinking we'd need eight, preferably ten, teams to pull it off."

"That was my assessment as well," Kilgore agreed.

"And you want to make it volunteers only? That's almost the entire detachment."

"I know. If we don't get enough signing up, we'll have to figure out another way."

Evans looked surprised. "Oh, they'll sign up. They'd follow you into the fires of Mako 7 if you asked them. The question is, what happens afterward when Bolivar finds out they went with you, knowing that you had been relieved of command?"

"Wait," Xin leaned forward. "Are you saying that the colonel shouldn't tell them? To protect them from the fallout?"

"I'm not saying that. I'm not *not* saying it either." Evans turned back to Kilgore. "I just want you to think through all the ramifications, sir."

Kilgore nodded and stroked the stubble on his chin thoughtfully. "I appreciate it, Keith. But I need to tell the troops. And I'll make sure they understand all the potential consequences. I'd rather they go in with their eyes wide open than under subterfuge."

Evans stood. "Well then. It's getting dark, and if we're going to make this work, we need to execute around two in the morning when the camp's night shift is most tired. That only gives us a day to prepare, so let's muster the men first thing in the morning and then get to briefing them."

"Wait?!" Feng asked in shock. "We're doing it tomorrow night?"

Kilgore smiled. "We have to move before Bolivar tracks us down and tries to stop us. He's probably realized we're gone by now, and it won't take him long to guess where I've gotten off to. He won't move on this camp immediately; he'll wait to gather enough men to hit us with overwhelming force—make us surrender out of fear without a fight. And fighting against our own forces right now would be a waste of time and lives on both sides. If he comes, we will surrender; there's no other way that can go.

"So, we have to move quickly, or this doesn't happen at all. We have all the gear in a nearby weapons cache. Now we just have to get the men and run through the op a few times so they all know their parts. In a pinch, we can do that in a day."

TWENTY-SEVEN
ACCIDENTAL MURDER
CAPTAIN KIMBERLEY PORTENOY, GPF

Kimberley Portenoy shook her head and let out a long sigh as she looked at the dead, broken body of Private Trevor Bentley. The man had been a troublemaker, but he'd been a member of her company, and even if he had sabotaged the mech like some were saying, he didn't deserve to die.

At least, there was no question as to who had done it. The sentries had found four mech drivers, writhing in pain, on the ground next to Bentley's body. It had been too late to save the private, but his attackers weren't going anywhere.

From their gasped confessions, under orders, of course, the four men had admitted attacking him in retaliation for the mech incident. They'd had no intention of killing him; their orders wouldn't allow for that anyway, and they were enacters. But things had gotten out of hand when Trevor pulled a knife and tried to defend himself. In the struggle that ensued, the knife had ended up in the private's own chest. It hadn't been an intentional murder, but that didn't matter to the four enacters, who were suffering the pain of disobedience now in the camp's stockade.

There was nothing the medics could do other than give them heavy painkillers. The agony would probably fade in time as the subconscious mind of each man reconciled what had happened. But for now, Kim was glad the men were in such pain. She'd even hinted to the medics to go easy on the morphine. They, like her, weren't enacters, and they were possibly annoyed by the imperious mech drivers just enough to at least consider it.

Now, though, Kim had other problems. Her entire company was awake and gathered in their barracks. And they were grumbling. Word had spread fast about what had happened to Private Bentley, and there was already talk of retaliation against the men in the stockade or the other mech drivers in the camp.

For much of Portenoy's company, who was already chafing at the friendly-fire incident with Corporal Tig and the general apathy and disdain of the mech drivers toward the lives of their 'softie' brothers and sisters in arms, taking revenge against any mech driver would do.

Worse, no one in her company was an enacter, so Kim wasn't sure she could stop them if they chose to take justice into their own hands.

She wasn't sure if she *wanted* to stop them.

TWENTY-EIGHT
MESSENGER
MAJOR KEITH EVANS, FCA

The messenger from Bolivar arrived sooner than Kilgore had even predicted. Before the sun even came up the next morning, an out-of-breath runner from the main command camp stopped at the checkpoint outside the special operations camp and, between gasps, told Major Evans that General Bolivar was ordering the arrest of Colonel Kilgore, Lieutenant Commander Xin Wang, and the Guard deserter Feng Chu Hua.

Evans rubbed the stubble on his chin thoughtfully. "Well, how about that?" he mused, eying the messenger, who was a full captain, not some private who had drawn the short straw like most. Obviously, Bolivar wanted someone with more authority delivering the message.

"I'll tell you what, Captain," he said in a friendly tone. "If I see the colonel or either of those other folks, I'll be sure to send them your way. But they're not here, and I haven't seen them."

The young captain looked at him incredulously. "The general said they would be here and that I wasn't to leave without taking them into custody and enlisting a few of your men to help guard them on the way back to command."

Evans shrugged. "Well, I don't know what to tell you, Captain.

They're not here. You're welcome to search the camp, if you'd like. But you won't find them here."

The man looked torn. And he looked past Evans to see Corporal Juarez, a tall, muscular woman covered in tattoos from head to toe, who was, at that moment, picking something out of her teeth with the tip of a nine-inch tactical knife. The woman winked at the man, who quickly turned his attention to another soldier sitting next to her at the checkpoint's small table. Staff Sergeant Federer looked the young officer in the eye as he casually snubbed out his cigar...on his own forearm, the odor of burning flesh filling the small tent.

The captain visibly gulped. "I suppose searching your camp is not necessary, Major, but if the fugitives do arrive here, I expect you will arrest them and send them to General Bolivar's camp first thing."

Evans smiled and clapped the young man on the shoulder. "Why sure, Captain. If I see them, you'll be the first to know. Do you want to stay for some breakfast before you head all the way back?"

He saw the young man look over again at where Juarez sat behind Evans. Whatever he saw made his eyes go wide, and he stammered, "N-no, sir. Thank you, sir. I best be on my way immediately."

He turned to go, but at the tent flap stopped and turned back. "One more thing. The last messenger sent to this camp never returned. Any chance he made it here last night?"

Evans pretended to think about it. The young man in question was under a friendly guard in the camp's interior, and the captain had to know that it wasn't a coincidence that the messenger had disappeared at the same time as Kilgore, Wang, and Feng. But the man seemed like he was just fishing at this point.

"No, haven't seen him. Lots of nasty things in the jungle though at night. General Bolivar really should be sending those messengers out in pairs at least."

The captain frowned but only nodded and then turned and left the tent. Evans stepped outside and watched him until he had entered the mouth of the long, winding path between the spec ops camp and Bolivar's command camp. When the officer was out of sight, he turned back and entered the tent again.

"Juarez, what did you do to that poor young man?" he asked in mock anger.

"Nuthin' Major," the corporal replied. "He was cute, so I was just flirtin'."

"She gave him her best come hither look," Federer said with a pained smirk. "She licked her lips and everything."

"He looked pretty delicious. What's a girl 'sposed to do to get a man in this jungle?" Juarez replied with a laugh.

"What's wrong with *you*, Sergeant?" Kilgore asked, turning his attention to the senior non-com. The man was shaking his arm and grimacing.

"That hurt, Major!" Federer replied, nodding toward the cigar burn on his arm. "I didn't join the snake eaters to feel pain like that."

"Well, then maybe you should sit out this mission," Evans observed dryly. "Might be too much risk of pain for your tender sensibilities."

"Nah, Major, I'll be good. So long as there's good coffee in that Guard camp. The swill here is slowly killing me; I know it."

It was Evans' turn to laugh. But then he stepped back out of the tent and looked after where the messenger had disappeared. Chewing on his lip, he shook his head. No matter what went down next, they were fully committed.

TWENTY-NINE
DEATH FROM ABOVE
CAPTAIN BOHDI PATEL, GPF

What happens when they do it again? What will I do?

Those two questions had been running through Bohdi Patel's head non-stop for the two days since he'd watched the mechs kill those 67 civilians. In his Guard Academy days, he remembered having discussions about situations like this in his ethics class. Back then, fresh off the farm and ready to begrudgingly save the galaxy, the class' theoretical discussions on ethical quandaries seemed almost trite to him. He could remember naively thinking that everyone with him in the class had simply accepted the need for ethics and morals as he did. Having an hour's worth of instruction three times a week on the subject felt like having a weekly lesson on how to tie your shoes. Everyone already knew how to do it, so why spend hours talking about it each week?

In his early years in the Guard, there had been little to disabuse him of that notion. Despite the forced way in which he'd been enlisted in the GPF, he'd quickly found a home there. After earning top marks in the two-year Guard Academy, he'd chosen to enroll immediately in Officer Candidate School. In the OCS's controlled environment, he had found little to suggest that any member of the Guard would willfully do something that wasn't for the greater good, and nothing had ever happened to cause him to question that assumption.

But then there had been that little scuffle on the asteroid eighteen months ago. One hundred and twenty-nine miners dead only because the mining company didn't want to give them a raise. At least, he had suspected that. But after a few hours of righteous indignation in which he'd planned a dozen different ways to call out his superior, Captain Houseman, for the massacre, he had lost his nerve. He'd started justifying what had happened. Maybe Houseman really thought the miners had indeed taken a hostage. Maybe the miners took advantage of the situation to make harsher demands. Maybe it was all just an honest mistake. Of course, a mere lieutenant—as he was at the time—wouldn't be read into all the details, so what did he really know?

So, in the end, 129 miners were dead, and Bohdi Patel said nothing.

But this time was different. Sixty-seven civilians were dead, and there was no justifying what had happened. Bohdi had been there, advised against it, and even turned down a direct order, but still, it had happened. And he was terrified it would happen again. He was even more terrified of what he would do *when* it happened again.

He didn't have to wait long to find out.

Two days after the incident with the apartment building, Bohdi and his company were clearing out the favelas in the northwest sector of San Sebastian. The favelas were the slums of Panamar, small shack-like homes literally stacked on top of each other and built into a steep hillside. Half-naked children ran through the streets, kicking soccer balls and throwing baseballs. Flea-bitten dogs followed them, and old men and women with missing teeth sat on rickety chairs, watching all of them and playing checkers and dominoes.

One of the mech squads had reported a platoon-size force of rebel soldiers that had fled from them and into the favelas a few hours before. The mechs couldn't pursue; the narrow alleyways and walkways on top of, around, and underneath the stacked homes precluded taking the large machines into the area. So, they had called for 'softie' support, and Bohdi's company, as that day's quick reaction force, had been airlifted in and set to the job of clearing the ghettos and warrens and finding the rebel soldiers.

It was an impossible task. The favelas were a maze that couldn't even be accurately mapped by the drones overhead, and no one knew what part the rebel force might be holed up in, assuming they hadn't already left the area through one of the many exits back into San Sebastian proper. For eight full hours, they had gone door-to-door, intruding upon sleeping infants, family meals, and everything in between, but with no sign of the rebel force.

They had found plenty of weapons, of course. Panamar had always had lax enforcement of the Council prohibition against civilians owning firearms. Given some of the things that lived in the jungles surrounding San Sebastian, it was near suicide to walk about unarmed, even at the edge of the city. So, the local Guard precincts had often looked the other way when it came to confiscating weapons and prosecuting those in possession of them.

But Bohdi had strict orders to confiscate any weapons his soldiers found, and by the end of just the first four hours, they had gathered too many to carry and had taken to sending runners back to the temporary command post to dump off one load after another.

However, even after eight hours, there was still no sign of the actual rebels. No one even took a potshot at Bohdi's troops. There had been a few instances of minor resistance, but nothing more than what one would expect of police searching a slum. They had interrupted a few drug deals and at least two acts of domestic violence, but it felt more like standard Guard policing work than an actual paramilitary operation.

Bohdi was about ready to call it and tell HQ that the rebel forces had most likely already moved on when a call came into his comm.

"Captain Patel?" a gruff voice asked. He reflexively stood at attention as his helmet holo identified the man.

"Yes, Colonel," he responded.

"Have you found that rebel platoon yet? You've certainly been at it for a while." By the tone, Bohdi knew what answer the man was looking for and that he was about to disappoint him.

"No, sir. No sign of them and no engagement. We believe they likely fled through the favelas and out to somewhere else in the city."

"Nonsense!" was the unexpected reply. "I can see on the drone footage that you've found quite a weapons cache in those slums."

Bohdi licked his lips. *Where is this going?* He weighed his next words carefully. "Sir, we have found weapons, but they appear to belong to civilians. Most of them are rusty old pistols and bolt-action rifles clearly printed at home. None of them match the parameters of the weapons we have observed the rebel forces using."

"That's a load of scud, Captain!" Colonel Klipinger snapped. "I'm looking at the footage now, and there are far too many weapons to be anything other than a cache for the rebellion. It's apparent to me, even if you can't see it, that those slums are a major rebel stronghold. And we need to take them out!"

Bohdi didn't reply for a moment, too stunned to speak. Finally, he found his voice again. "Uh...sir, take who out?"

"The rebels, obviously!" the older man snapped. "I have orders directly from General Nissen to eliminate any aid and support the rebels may be getting in the northwest sector. And that means eliminating those that are giving them support, supplies, and weapons!"

"With all due respect, Colonel," Bohdi argued, though a sinking feeling told him it was a doomed effort, "we have seen zero indication that the rebels are operating in the favelas. Everything points to the people here being unconnected to them." That wasn't entirely true—Bohdi doubted there was a single part of the city that wasn't aiding the rebels in some way, but he didn't like where this conversation was going.

"Captain, if you're not willing to do what needs to be done, I will relieve you of command and find someone else who will do their duty! Is that understood?"

Bohdi shook his head in shock. "Y-yes, sir. Understood," was all he could think to say.

"Good, I am ordering you to clear your troops out of the area now. We will be using alternative measures to clear it. You have fifteen minutes to get your men and women clear of that sector, Captain. Now get on it!"

"But, sir—" Bohdi started to argue again, but Colonel Klipinger had already cut the comm channel.

Bohdi quickly relayed the order to get out of the favelas to all of his troops on the Tac Net and assigned Lieutenant Lindstrom to coordinate the evac and to call him immediately if there were any problems. Then he opened up a new comm channel.

"Major Rodriguez! Listen, I just spoke with the colonel, and—"

"I know, Captain," she cut him off, her voice subdued. "Listen, just follow your orders and get your people out of there as quickly as possible."

"What's going to happen, Major?" He knew he sounded out of breath and desperate, but he just didn't care in that moment.

"Listen, Bohdi," she replied, her voice reminding him of a grade-school teacher he'd once had. "They're sending in the dropships."

"But, we're not..." He had been about to say that they weren't yet done with their patrol shift, so there was no need to bring the company back to base, but then the import of it hit him. "They're going to carpet bomb the area?" His voice was like a whisper as if the words were too difficult to say any louder.

"Bohdi, just get your people out of there."

"But Major—Tiff—we can't let this happen. There aren't even any rebels here! They're just innocents!"

"Bohdi, stop!" her voice was sharp, though it broke just a small bit. "The decision has been made. General Nissen ordered it personally."

"But why?" he pleaded.

"Think about it. You know why."

And he did. Nissen was an enacter. So was Klipinger. It was literally impossible to get to their lofty ranks without the genetic mutation. No one wanted a senior officer who could disobey orders. That meant that the order had come from above, or...

"They're trying to save face, aren't they? The rebels have been beating up the infantry. They have to show that they can be as effective as the mechs."

"Bohdi, careful." He hadn't even realized he'd said the words out loud and frantically checked to make sure that the channel with Rodriguez was secure. It was.

"But Tiff, this is wrong. We have to stop it! There are thousands of civilians in those slums. Children, Tiff. Children!"

"Bohdi, I have to go. Just get your people out of there." And the connection went dead.

Bohdi Patel suddenly found himself at an inflection point—one he had never expected to be at. He couldn't stop what was about to happen, but he could do *something*.

Keying an open channel to his entire company on the Tac Net, he said the words he knew would end his Guard career. "Easy Company, listen up! There are dropships inbound to carpet bomb the favelas. Keep moving out of the area; you have eight minutes. But I'm ordering you to tell every civilian you see on the way out to evacuate. Tell them to get out now!"

He watched the seconds tick by, then the minutes. Twice, he tried to call Rodriguez back, but she wasn't answering. He tried to call Colonel Klipinger, but there was no answer. With three minutes to go, he put in a call to the command center emergency line and argued with a major there, demanding to speak with everyone all the way to General Nissen before the man simply hung up on him.

He watched helplessly on the Tac Net as drone footage showed the green dots of his soldiers all clearing the designated target area. Blue dots representing civilians milled about, some of them following his men and women out, but most scurrying around as if they were gathering possessions or loved ones. In the center of the area—the parts his troops had left first, before his order to warn the populace—the word-of-mouth message was slow to arrive, and by the time he saw the people there start to move about, he knew none of them had a chance to make it out.

A whine in the distance caught his attention, and he zoomed out the Tac Net map to see the large green outlines of four dropships moving at speed toward the slums. In one last desperate attempt, he ordered his helmet computer to open a comm channel with the lead dropship's pilot.

"Dropship 412B, this is Captain Bohdi Patel on the ground at the target area. Friendlies in the target area. I repeat, friendlies in the target area. Abort! Abort! Abort!"

"No can do, Captain," the response came. "Tac Net shows all friendlies clear of the area, and we have our orders."

Bohdi's heart raced. The man was probably an enacter, so his orders would trump anything Bohdi could say to him, but he *had* to try. He keyed into his holo a command to expand the channel to include the pilots of all four dropships. "Dropship Element B, this is Captain Bohdi Patel. There are no rebels in the target area. Civilians only! I repeat, there are only civilians in the target area. Abort your bombing run! Abort!"

He practically screamed the last, but his heart sank further as none of the dropships acknowledged his pleas. His comm abruptly screamed static at him, and his Tac Net holo disappeared. Then, a new voice spoke in his helmet.

"Captain Patel, this is Major Youst with Command Central. You are relieved of command and ordered to remain at Command Post 14 and remand yourself into the custody of Internal Affairs officers, who will be arriving shortly. Do you acknowledge?"

Bohdi said nothing but watched in shocked despair. With his access to the Tac Net cut off, he could no longer see the overhead map of the target area, but from his command post's vantage on a nearby hill, he could see the four dropships screaming toward it over the rooftops. At the last second, one of the four dropships peeled off, and he felt a moment of hope. But his hope was shattered when the remaining three ships began dropping their munitions, and the favelas and tens of thousands of civilian lives still inside them vanished in roiling balls of fire.

THIRTY
VOLUNTEERS
COLONEL SAM KILGORE, FCA

After the men and women of his special ops detachment had eaten breakfast, Kilgore approached them all unit by unit and told them about his plan to raid the Guard command camp. He had chosen to speak with them in smaller groups so that they would be more comfortable asking questions and less likely to agree to the plan just because of peer pressure.

But in the end, all 144 men and women in the special ops detachment, plus all of their officers, volunteered to take part in the raid. They had the manpower they needed and, an hour afterward had the equipment and the weaponry from a nearby cache. They spent the rest of the day going over the finer points of the plan, making adjustments based on feedback from the officers and senior non-coms, and generally getting ready to go.

Chu Hua and Xin spent the time recording and editing the message they planned to send out to the planet, the Guard, and the fleet in orbit. They had run the final contents by Kilgore, Evans, and one of their captains, who was something akin to a psyops warfare specialist and had several suggestions. In the end, they all felt the final product had the best shot of accomplishing their goals.

Later, as they were eating dinner, one of their outer pickets came running back into the camp. "It's Bolivar!" he said to Kilgore, barely breathing hard despite having run a full two kilometers back at speed through thick jungle. "He's sent two companies our way. He must not have bought what Major Evans told that messenger."

Kilgore frowned. "I didn't expect he would. Alright," he turned to the other officers in the command tent, "you heard the man. We have maybe five or ten minutes before this place is crawling with Bolivar's men. Let's get going!"

Twelve minutes later, when the forward elements of the force Juan Bolivar had sent to capture Colonel Kilgore and his companions entered the special operations camp, they found it completely deserted, save for one tied-up young messenger, the remains of a half-eaten dinner evident everywhere they looked.

―――

Major Gonzalo Huerta, FCA

Major Gonzalo Huerta shook his head as he surveyed the empty camp. One of his men handed him something, and he looked down to find a piece of old-style paper. On it was a short note:

Sorry we weren't here to welcome you. Gone hunting! Feel free to finish up dinner for us, but would you mind doing the dishes while you're here?

Despite himself, Huerta shook his head and laughed, drawing a few confused looks from the men and women under his command.

"Anybody got a pen?" he called out to his troops.

A moment later, someone pressed one into his hand, and he nodded his thanks. Below the note left for them, he wrote his reply.

Next time, invite us to dinner before you start eating. And you can clean up your own mess!

"Sir, what's so funny?" Captain Gregori asked as he saw his major chuckling to himself.

"Nothing Gregori. Tell the men we're heading back to camp. There's nothing for us here."

THIRTY-ONE
STOCKADE
CAPTAIN BOHDI PATEL, GPF

Bohdi sat on the hard cot, which was the only piece of furniture in the small stockade that was set up in the Guard camp. He was alone there, occupying one of the only three cells, but he knew there were similar buildings elsewhere in the forward operating base. He had spent the night in his small cell and had been too disconsolate to eat dinner but was now picking through the meager and overcooked breakfast his guards had brought him.

While he tried to chew through a piece of what he thought was supposed to be ham, he heard the outer door to the stockade open and footsteps approaching.

"Leave us," a female voice said, and he heard the two guards acknowledge the order and leave through the same door. He looked up to see Major Tiffany Rodriguez standing outside the bars of his cell and looking down at him with a pained expression.

"How are they treating you?" she asked, though the question felt pro forma.

He shrugged and gestured down at the breakfast. "The accommodations are fine, but I have notes for the chef." He tried to inject a cavalier levity into his tone but knew he failed miserably.

Rodriguez frowned and shook her head. "Can't you take anything seriously? This is not good, Bohdi. Not at all. What did you even hope to accomplish?"

He felt the blood rush to his face and gritted his teeth to stop the first words he thought of from coming out. Then he angrily tossed the breakfast tray to the hard ground, making Rodriguez jump in surprise.

"What was I supposed to do, Tiff? What would you have done? Thousands, maybe tens of thousands, of civilians dead, and for what? So that Nissen and Klipinger can look like they're doing something when they go to dinner with the mech staff officers? Or so that their enacter gene doesn't give them a headache? What was I supposed to do? Just let it happen? Let them kill children for the sake of their own puffed-up egos?"

"Shut up, Bohdi!" Her angry tone surprised him enough to stop his rant. "They're going to court-martial you! Can't you get that through that thick skull of yours? You're done as a guardsman, and you'll be lucky not to get the death penalty. That's what Nissen and Klipinger are pushing for!"

It took a moment for the words to sink in, but Bohdi was surprised that they didn't hurt as bad as they could have. "Tiff, listen. If the Guard is an organization that kills innocent children so that a bunch of enacters can tell themselves they're following their orders, then I don't want to be a part of it.

"I did what I did, and a few extra people survived. I can live or die with that."

"And what about the dropship pilot you subverted? He's in the next stockade over, by the way, and he's facing a court-martial, too. Did you stop to think about what might happen to him? Poor guy can't even eat; he's in so much pain from disobeying his orders."

Bohdi smiled. "I'm sorry he's getting punished and that he's in so much pain, but I'm glad he listened to me. At least two of us can sleep well for the remaining time we have left. How are you sleeping these days, Tiff?"

To his surprise, her answer wasn't another lecture but a genuine look of pain and even the wet glisten of tears forming in her eyes. Her next words were in a pleading tone. "Bohdi, listen to me. I've told them you've been under a lot of stress lately. I told them you came to me and complained of nightmares and panic attacks from combat. That everything you did was just part of a mental breakdown. It's the only thing I could think of to get you off. They'll still kick you out of the Guard, but you might live through this."

As she spoke of what she'd done, sticking her own neck out to save him, Bohdi felt no gratitude, but a surprising anger welled up inside him. He stood up and moved to the bars so that he was looking her straight in the face, and she had to crane her neck to look up at his taller frame.

"Don't cheapen what I did out there, Tiff. Don't do it!" he growled. "I knew *exactly* what I was doing, and I would do it again. Go back and tell them that. I want them to know that there's at least someone here who will stand up to them. I want them looking over their shoulders every time they give an order, wondering if someone like me will tell them where to shove it. That's the only way they might reconsider what they're doing here, and Council knows where else.

"I'm sick of watching innocent people die, and I want them to know that. Someone has to tell them it's wrong!"

Tiffany was crying openly now and shaking her head in denial. "No, Bohdi, you don't mean that. Don't do this! There has to be another way. They'll kill you, don't you get that? You'll be dead, and then all of your noble objections won't mean a thing. Live, Bohdi. You need to live. *I* need you to live."

He reached through the bars and gently put his hands on her shoulders, then moved his right hand to cradle her chin and lift her face back up to look at his. "Tiff, I...I can't. Not even for you. I might live, but it wouldn't be the kind of life I want to have. I'm sorry."

She stepped back, out of his reach, and hastily dried her eyes with the sleeves of her jungle fatigues. "I guess that's it then," she practically whispered. "I tried to save you, Bohdi. I really did."

She turned before he could respond and left through the outer door. A moment later, it opened again, and he heard multiple sets of footsteps approaching. Expecting his guards, he was surprised to see Lieutenants Lindstrom, McAfee, Martinez, and Herdaz, the four platoon commanders from his company.

"Hey, Cap," Lupe Martinez said as the three men and one woman stopped in front of his cell. "Major told the guards to let us talk to you alone for a few minutes."

Bohdi wanted to shake his head. He was already feeling conflicted for the way he'd told off Tiffany, and here she was, still trying to help him out. "It's good to see you all, but I would suggest distancing yourselves from me as much as possible right now. I'm as radioactive as they come."

"Not gonna do it, Cap," McAfee said around the toothpick he habitually chewed on. "You're gonna beat this, and we're gonna help you."

Bohdi shook his head. "Not this time. This time, I've really stepped in it. Don't let your careers go down with mine. Please." He immediately noted the irony of feeling fine taking down the career of some faceless enacter dropship pilot but desperately wanting the men and women in his own command to stay out of it.

"Cap, we have a plan," said Lindstrom conspiratorially. "We're not letting them kill you for this."

"Whatever it is, put it out of your mind now!" he replied sharply, and the young man jerked back in surprise. "No way I want to go to the gallows with the lives of you four idiots on my conscience, too." He knew he was being too harsh, but he had to get through to them, just like Tiffany had tried to get through to him. "Just drop it and do whatever Major Rodriguez tells you to, understood?"

"Yes, sir," came a chorus of reluctant voices, and Bohdi could tell he hadn't quite dissuaded them yet.

He opened his mouth to try again when the outer stockade door opened once more, and the gruff voice of one of the Internal Affairs guardsmen intruded. "Visiting time is over, sirs. I need to ask you to leave."

Lindstrom winked at him as the four turned to go, and Bohdi shook his head in desperation, but the man pretended not to notice. When they were gone, he slumped back on his cot and looked morosely at the breakfast scattered on his cell floor.

PART FOUR
ENDGAME

THIRTY-TWO
MARCH
EX-PRIVATE FENG CHU HUA, GPF DESERTER

It was a five-hour march through the jungle to the Guard's command camp, and Kilgore estimated they would arrive by around 11:30 pm. They had set the attack time at 1:30 am, far enough ahead of the 2:00 am changing of the sentries that the outgoing sentries would be at their most tired and the incoming wouldn't yet be fully awake in their barracks.

Even Xin and Chu Hua would take part in the attack, though in more of a support role, and to make sure Chu Hua's message could go out even if the multiple recorded copies carried by various infiltrators didn't survive the mission.

With such a small force against so large of one, they knew their odds were long, but there was no hesitation or reluctance in the groups of special ops troops who glided silently through the jungle, making Chu Hua feel like every step she took echoed through the damp air by comparison.

"Are we just sending these men and women to their deaths?" she whispered to Xin Wang, who trudged along just as noisily next to her.

He stopped, grabbing her arm so that she had to stop as well and face him. Spec ops troops moved around the new obstacle they represented without complaint or additional noise.

"You have to stop thinking like that," Xin whispered back. "You're a miracle, you know that? You did what only two others have done in a millennium of recorded history. And you did it for the right reasons. *Everyone* on this planet, in orbit, and in the galaxy needs to know your story and Sergeant Nowak's.

"One time is an aberration, and Tyrus Tyne isn't around to defend the counter-narrative the Council has put out to deny the story of him going rogue. But with it happening again, and more witnesses to the fact, it will be *a lot* harder for the Council to continue to deny the Revelations.

"Sarah Nowak is dead, and by your own account, the powers that be are likely to make sure her story never gets out.

"You're alive, and you can get your story out and Sarah's, and you'll be alive later to fight the counter-narrative that is sure to go out. They can keep denying what you say, but you are the ultimate evidence, a living, breathing enacter who can clearly stand up and show the galaxy that she is *not* obedient to the Council or anyone else anymore through simple genetics. Do you understand how valuable that is to the cause of freedom?"

Throughout his speech, Chu Hua had been looking down at her shoes, feeling the blood rushing to her face as he put so much on her shoulders, and feeling the headache that came whenever she thought of what she'd done. But when he was done talking, she forced her spine straight and lifted herself to her full diminutive height to look up and right into his eyes.

"I understand, but I need to know that you'll be there with me. Both to support me and in case the pain of going back is too much and I somehow can't fight my genetics anymore."

Xin smiled and reached down to grab Chu Hua's hand, holding it lightly. "Just try and stop me," he whispered.

Hours later, as they neared the Guard's forward operating base for the invasion of Panamar, they still walked hand-in-hand. And the warmth of Xin's hand in hers somehow deadened the pain.

THIRTY-THREE
BASE
COLONEL SAM KILGORE, FCA

"Private Feng's intel was spot on. The Guard here are pretty lax. I've watched two of the on-duty sentries chatting for the last 45 minutes. They looked out at the jungle maybe twice and probably would have missed a tetrapuma walking right up to them. Their night vision is worthless because they never leave the light, and they don't even have lights illuminating more than a few meters past their perimeter. They were even considerate enough to flash clear most of the trees on the perimeter for us so that that crazy pilot's plan might actually work."

Kilgore nodded at the report from Master Sergeant Gil Lorre, his senior NCO and best scout. "Any complications?"

Lorre nodded. "Just one that I saw, plus another that Ruiz noticed. Like I said, the Guard is pretty lax here; I'm sure they can't imagine someone actually hitting them in their own camp. Almost all the sentries are regs or mech drivers without their rigs. But there are two mechs roaming the perimeter on a 30-minute cycle. Predictable, but either one could cause real problems for us if we don't take them out on the first try."

"How likely is it we get them on the first try?" The question was one that, by rights, Kilgore himself should have been answering as the mission commander, but he trusted Lorre and the man's quick brain and wanted to hear his unfiltered opinion.

The master sergeant shrugged his beefy shoulders. "We have the weapons, and those clankers make so much noise stomping around the perimeter that we will have no problem knowing exactly where they are when it's go time. But a lot can happen. Still, I put it at 75% or better."

Kilgore nodded appreciatively. Lorre's assessment was actually a little more optimistic than his own. "You mentioned two problems. What's the second one? The one Ruiz noticed."

Lorre frowned. "Drones. He heard two of the guardsmen talking, and they mentioned clearly that they have overwatch drones above the camp, watching for incursions and streaming real-time imagery to the Guard Tac Net. It's probably part of why they're so lax on the human aspect of sentry duty. But that also means that as soon as we break the cover of the surrounding jungle, they're likely to see us and raise the alarm, even if the human response is slow."

"Can we take the drones out?"

The man shook his head. "Not without knowing exactly where they are. But if they are flying low and using thermals, which is most likely at night, then their field of view is going to be limited, and we may be able to hide some of our numbers by sticking close to and in between the buildings where our thermals might get muddled or confused by the occupants of the barracks and duty posts. Along with the general back-scatter the latent warmth in the soil throws off, it might at least confuse the response even if the alarm goes off."

"OK. Make the rounds and tell the troops we go in twenty from my mark. Get two crews assigned to shadow each mech and be ready to take it out. And hold back a squad with search-and-destroy rockets to take out those drones the second they get any indication of where they are."

Lorre raised his watch, a special model like the rest of the rebel spec ops troops had that wasn't connected to Panamar's meager planetary network, and that didn't transmit any signals unless he chose to. On Kilgore's signal, he started a timer and then dashed off into the undergrowth to pass along Kilgore's orders by word of mouth; it was far too risky to use their comms this close to the Guard camp.

Kilgore turned back to look at the lights of the Guard forward operating base, visible even through 50 meters of thick jungle. He frowned. Men and women under his command would die this night, and that would be on his conscience for the rest of his life. He only hoped it was worth it.

THIRTY-FOUR
ATTACK
PRIVATE LIM, GPF

Private Lim was *so* tired. He was also annoyed. His company had been planning to get back at the mech drivers who had killed Trevor Bentley, and he wanted very much to be part of their plans. Instead, he was stuck on the outside perimeter in the most worthless sentry post that had ever been devised.

He was looking toward the interior of the camp, wondering when his mates would be making their move, and had no warning before he felt someone grab him from behind. Lim had just enough time to feel the cold metal against his neck before his world went dark.

Sergeant Tina Montescu, FCA

Sergeant Tina Montescu raised the odd-looking contraption and used the built-in scope to aim it. From her perch in the upper branches of the bantara tree, she pulled the trigger, and a monofilament line shot out behind a titanium alloy arrow. It flew straight and true, with the right amount of drop, and impacted solidly with a tree that rose in the middle of the Guard camp—one of the few they hadn't cut down to make room for their barracks and other temporary structures.

Reaching up to the line, Tina affixed her trolley. The other end of the trolley assembly was already attached to the harness she wore, and the other end of the monofilament line was anchored to the tree in which she perched.

Checking her watch, she counted down the seconds and then triggered the anti-grav belt she wore—it would take just enough of her weight off the thin line that it wouldn't bend as much, and she would stay high above the barracks buildings. And the trolley had an electric motor that would speed her along as soon as the clock reached zero.

Lieutenant Todd Hodges, GPF

"Sir, the perimeter drones are flagging aberrant heat signatures on the edges of the FOB!" called one of the corporals inside the small sensor shack. Lieutenant Todd Hodges couldn't remember the woman's name.

"Probably just wildlife, like always, Corporal," he said in a bored voice, sipping from his coffee and going back to the less-than-savory novel he was reading on his pad.

"No, sir," the woman insisted. "It's definitely people. And at least a few dozen. Are we expecting any pre-dawn patrols returning or transfers from any of the other bases?"

Todd looked up from his pad and scrunched up his face in confusion. "Not that I'm aware of. Let me call the Command Center and see."

"Sir, I think maybe we need to sound the alarm." The woman's voice was timid, but she wasn't letting it go.

Todd sighed and looked at the physical button at his station that would sound the alarm throughout the camp. The last officer who had sounded that alarm—it had been a false alert, a sentry mistaking another sentry for an enemy infiltrator the first week on Panamar—had gotten demoted by General Ostertag after being reamed by every officer in the man's chain of command.

Private JC Rawlins, GPF

An alarm sounded, reverberating through the camp in a rising and falling tone that jerked Private JC Rawlins from a half-doze into an instant, confused awareness. He looked around frantically for any sign of intruders around his sentry post.

But the attack that took out Private Rawlins wasn't from any of the places he looked. A silenced shot from almost directly above lodged itself in JC's brain before he knew what was happening.

Captain Bohdi Patel, GPF

The alarm also jerked Bohdi awake in his cell and he looked around in near panic.

"What's going on?" he called to the two guards who always manned the stockade, but all he heard was the sound of rushing feet and the opening of the outer door. For a brief second, he heard the sound of men and women shouting and the discharge of several weapons before the door shut behind the fleeing guards, and the sounds were muffled.

He started to look around desperately for something, anything, that would get him out of the cell, but the only thing outside the cot and his own clothes was the toilet that was affixed solidly to the floor. He was stuck! And whatever was happening outside, it didn't sound like a drill.

The sirens and yelling got abruptly louder again as the door to the stockade was flung open again. Bohdi leapt to the wall of his cell, hiding against it where whoever was coming down the short hall wouldn't see him until they had completely passed by the previous cell. If he could surprise them through the bars...

A familiar face came into view, and Bohdi relaxed, though only a little.

"Lindstrom, what's going on out there?"

"Dunno Cap," the young lieutenant said, his voice shaky. "Lots of alarms and yelling, something about an attack maybe, but nothing clear."

"What are you doing out and about at this hour?"

"Well, I was coming to get you out. We were trying to figure out a way to distract your guards when everything went to hell." Bohdi could see that the young man was literally shaking.

"OK. OK. Calm down a bit. Do you have a way to get me out of here? Maybe I can help with whatever's going on."

"Oh, yeah." The young man looked embarrassed and pulled a device out of his pocket. It was a standard Guard lock pick gun, used when they wanted to breach a building but do it quietly.

Lindstrom set to work on the lock on Bohdi's cell. It was electronic, but the gun had a digital setting that could hack and open all but the most sophisticated doors. After a few moments, which seemed to stretch into eternity as Bohdi listened to the muffled shouts and gunfire from outside, the lock clicked open.

He quickly and wordlessly followed Lindstrom out into the hall, and the two men stood by the door. On Bohdi's silent count of three, the lieutenant pulled the door open, and they rushed outside and into utter bedlam.

Sergeant Tina Montescu, FCA

Tina rode the monofilament like an old comic book she'd seen of a flying superhero. The harness she wore attached at the back to the zip line's trolley, and her belly faced down toward the Guard camp. She sighted through her carbine's thermal scope and took out another sentry before the man even thought to look up.

She knew that around her, another roughly twenty spec ops troops were taking similar flights through the camp.

The sentries taken care of, her path led her over one of the barracks buildings. As she flew over it, she removed an item from her belt and dropped it onto the top of the temporary structure.

About ten seconds later, after she'd dropped three more of the objects on other structures below her, she felt the heat and saw the flash of light behind her as the first of the charges exploded. The small grenade-like bombs wouldn't destroy the structures or even necessarily hurt the occupants, but they would drive enough confusion and even panic to slow down the response to the rebel spec ops attack.

She smiled as more charges exploded, and she raised her gun to take out an officer who had stepped outside one of the cylindrical command structures near the center of the camp. Despite the danger, this was a lot more fun than she'd expected.

Lieutenant Jose Sandoval, GPF

Sandoval raced toward the mech depot. Around him, men yelled, and explosions rocked the night. He had no idea who was attacking the camp, but it seemed like they were everywhere, even though he had yet to actually see one of the attackers.

An explosion blew out the top of a barracks building as he was running by it, sending rubble flying in all directions. A piece of plasticrete hit Jose in the hip and knocked him to the ground.

He looked up from the dirt in a daze, his ears ringing from the sound of the blast and his hip hurting sharply, but a small part of his brain stayed lucid enough to wonder why the explosion had come from the *top* of the barracks.

Master Sergeant Gil Lorre, FCA

Master Sergeant Lorre ran, no weapon in hand, but with false panic toward the center of the camp, away from the explosions and the shooting. Dozens of men and women ran around him, all in Guard uniforms matching the fake one he wore, some heading in the same direction—away from the action—and a smaller number running toward the outskirts of the camp where they thought all of the attackers must be.

Lorre resisted the urge to smile. He and a few others had entered the camp several minutes before the rest of the special forces team had made their move. The rebel soldiers attacking from the jungle and the zip-lining operators causing bedlam throughout the camp were merely a sideshow. Lorre and the other scouts were the real mission.

Nearing his objective, he slowed his run and surreptitiously looked around. He spotted one of the other scouts about ten meters away, and the two carefully avoided eye contact. There were eight infiltrators in all, entering the camp from multiple directions, all alone, and all wearing some of the very few and very expensive thermal-blocking bodysuits that the rebels had under their fake Guard uniforms.

Now Lorre was at his target. He reached down to his belt and removed a small object clipped to it. It looked like a portable comm, just like those worn by many of the guardmembers running throughout the camp. Now, he smiled as he reached up and affixed the fake comm to the side of the comm jamming tower in the middle of the camp.

His work done, he turned heel and ran, again faking the same panic as so many others around him, but now heading toward the comm shack fifty meters away.

THIRTY-FIVE
BROADCAST
COLONEL SAM KILGORE, FCA

Sam Kilgore, Feng Chu Hua, and Xin Wang hurried through the camp. Like the scouts, they wore Guard uniforms, though Chu Hua's was actually real. Kilgore was dressed as a Guard paramilitary captain, and Chu Hua and Xin both looked the part of privates. Feng wore her hat pulled low over her face so that she was less likely to be recognized by any of her former colleagues.

They made their way rapidly toward the comm shack. As they ran, Kilgore checked his watch.

"Down!" he cried, and he dove to the ground, trusting that Xin and Chu Hua would do likewise. Just as he hit the dirt, an explosion rocked the camp as seven of the eight charges the scouts had been sent to plant on the jamming tower exploded simultaneously—the eighth scout had been discovered and killed, almost by accident.

"Jammers are down!" he cried back to Feng and Wang on the ground behind him. The special earpieces they wore had protected their hearing from the explosion.

Without waiting for them to reply, he leapt back up to his feet and started running, now at full sprint, to the comm shack. He spied Lorre and two of the other scouts already poised to enter the building.

When he and the others arrived, along with three more scouts, the now eight-strong team rushed through the door, pistols drawn—carrying anything larger would have made them stand out from the other confused guardmembers running throughout the camp.

Inside the shack, they found only one lone junior officer. Kilgore guessed that the rest of the normal occupants were outside trying to mount a defense against the rebel attackers. The poor young man should have surrendered quickly in the face of eight soldiers with drawn weapons, but he made a desperate grab for his sidearm, and Lorre shot him twice through the head.

Probably an enacter, Kilgore thought grimly. Ordered never to surrender. Or maybe he was just stupid.

Either way, the comm officer was dead, and the six special forces operators, plus a pilot and a traitorous mech driver, were alone in the shack controlling the Guard's most powerful on-planet transmitters.

Kilgore smiled. "Master Sergeant, let's get this thing fired up and get Private Feng's message to the masses."

Lieutenant Jose Sandoval, GPF

Jose Sandoval had finally made it to the mech depot, only to find the chaos from outside was also inside. Reports were rolling in from across the camp. But they were a jumbled mess: stories of phantom invaders, some even *flying* around at treetop level. Still, all seemed to agree that someone had blown up the jamming tower. He also hadn't been able to raise the two mechs that were supposed to be patrolling the camp perimeter.

About a dozen mech operators—only a dozen out of the hundreds in the camp—had made it to the depot. Four of them were almost done suiting up, but the rest were still prepping their mechs. The massive machines took a full fifteen minutes to go from cold to operational, and only five minutes, give or take, had passed since Jose had first become aware of the attack.

He grabbed a passing tech, forcing the man to look him in the eyes. "What about the sentry mechs? Have they reported in?"

The tech shook his head and slipped Sandoval's grasp to run and prep another mech. Jose threw up his hands in exasperation and grabbed his belt comm to try and raise the patrolling mechs again.

"Sentries One and Two, report!"

He waited, hearing no response. He tried again and again, but no one replied. Finally, his comm crackled, and a voice practically shouted from the speaker. "This is Private Lopez on the south side! Both mechs are down. They had some sort of missile launchers!"

Jose let the comm drop and hung his head in frustration. He looked back up at the frenetic activity all around him and had a sinking feeling that it was all too little too late. By the time the mechs were ready to roll, it would all be over.

"Attention citizens of Panamar and guardmembers on the planet and in orbit. This is Private Feng Chu Hua of the 4th Light Mechanized Division, 17th Platoon, 2nd Squad. My Guard authentication code is..."

The voice came out of Sandoval's comm and the comms of every other guardmember in the building, as well as through the PA speakers in each corner of the depot's interior.

Sandoval looked down at his comm in horror. *No!*

Captain Kimberley Portenoy, GPF

Kimberley pulled up from her mad dash across the camp and stared in shock at the comm in her hand. She'd never met the almost juvenile-sounding woman speaking from the device, but the authentication number would prove she was legitimate to every Guard wearing their watch who could run a quick check as she did now.

"*I am speaking to you now to share my story of how I overcame my enacter mutation and disobeyed the orders of my officers. But first, I want to share the story of Sergeant Sarah Nowak, who bravely...*"

Captain Bohdi Patel, GPF

Bohdi stopped running and held out a hand to stop Lindstrom next to him. They'd been joined by McAfee, Martinez, and Herdaz shortly after leaving the stockade and had been making their way to one of the armories to grab something bigger than the sidearms the four lieutenants wore.

"Listen!" he called out. "What is that?"

"Feng," replied Lupe Martinez. "Say, wasn't there some mech private that went missing named that?"

Bohdi shushed her and listened carefully to the message that seemed to be coming from every speaker, watch, and comm in the camp.

"Sergeant Nowak bravely shot herself so that she wouldn't have to follow an order to commit a war crime—to kill an innocent baby—because her commanding officers thought they could order her to do anything, and that, as an enacter, she would have no choice but to comply. You've all seen the terrible things they've been commanding the mech drivers to do. Just two days ago, they destroyed an apartment building with over sixty innocent civilians inside. They wanted Sarah to do the same thing.

"But they didn't know Sarah like I did. She was a loyal enacter but also a loving wife and mother. And she..."

Sub-Commander George Cornwall, GSF

Guard Sub-Commander George Cornwall listened in shock to the spritely young voice coming through the bridge comm on the Guard Heavy Cruiser *Solstice* that hung in orbit around Panamar. His mouth was hanging open and had been since the woman's first words had emanated from the cruiser's bridge speakers.

"...she refused her orders. She refused to kill the innocent people in that apartment building. Unlike the other mech drivers, who refuse to even question their orders, Sarah refused to kill that baby. She may have been an enacter, but she made a choice. It was a difficult one, and it killed her, but it was her choice.

"I made a choice too..."

Captain Bohdi Patel, GPF

"...and my choice was to desert rather than be part of the system that killed my friend Sarah Nowak. The pain was intense at first, but it was worth every second of it..."

Bohdi looked at the four slack-jawed lieutenants with him.

"Do you think it's true, Cap?" Huerta asked, his eyes wide. "Can enacters really disobey if they want to bad enough?"

Bohdi just shook his head slowly. He had no answers for the man, but a growing anger was rising in his chest.

"Call the company. Tell them to meet us at the command center. Go! Now!" Immediately, his four underlings started poking at their watch holos. And Bohdi realized belatedly that he had just turned his entire company into traitors along with him.

Captain Kimberley Portenoy, GPF

Kimberley listened in rapt attention to the words of Private Feng Chu Hua as she spoke of the arrogance of the Guard enacter leadership and how they'd taken advantage of Sarah Nowak, Feng, and other enacters to commit crimes against humanity, all in the name of suppressing the rebellion by any means necessary.

She thought of Corporal Tig and Private Trevor Bentley, and a rage rose inside of her.

Sub-Commander George Cornwall, GSF

"I have met many members of the rebellion, one who personally met Tyrus Tyne, the enacter and alpha who first defied the Council government. On top of that, I have learned to my satisfaction that the Revelations and all that they tell us are true. The Council is a lie; the Keeper and his cronies were responsible for the destruction of Rinali Station, all to turn us against the Four Worlds. And they are still

working to turn all of the citizens of the 47 Colonies into enacters. Even more, they—"

"What is the meaning of this?! Cut off that transmission!" The authoritative voice of Guard Commander Jasper Hewitt boomed from the open hatch into the *Solstice's* bridge. Sub-Commander Cornwall turned to see his captain, red in the face, glaring at him.

"Captain, is it true?" The question didn't come from Cornwall but from Lieutenant Harriet Nunes, the sensor officer.

"Nothing but lies!" Hewitt yelled, spittle flying from his lips.

"Liar!" Cornwall was surprised to hear his own voice rising in anger. In his mind, a moment from his childhood played over and over: his own mother being dragged from his home when he was just four years old, right before they'd taken him to the Enacter Academy. He had never understood why she'd been taken until years later when his father had made contact and told him she'd protested the Council taking *him* away at such a young age. She *hadn't* been an enacter—like his father, she carried only the recessive gene, but she *had* been put in prison for crimes against the Council. Just as Cornwall was about to graduate from the Guard Academy, he'd learned she'd been killed in a prison fight that had always felt a little too convenient, coming just weeks before her supposed release date.

As an enacter, Cornwall had never thought he could do anything about it—even question it consciously—but suddenly...

Suddenly, with the words of a young woman he'd never met, he felt free!

Captain Hewitt still stood there, gaping at his executive officer's outburst and fumbling for his sidearm, when Sub-Commander George Cornwall forcibly pushed aside the sharp pain in his temple, raised his own sidearm, and shot the man through the head.

Turning to the rest of the bridge crew, none of them who were enacters, Cornwall said, "Rebel. Resist. Don't listen to the lies." Then, the pain too great for him to bear, he collapsed to the deck and blacked out. His last conscious thought was: *I never liked the Captain anyway.*

Major Tiffany Rodriguez, GPF

Major Rodriguez listened in shock to the words issuing from every speaker, large and small, in the armory. Around her, dozens of guardmembers, most of them halfway through strapping on body armor and tactical helmets, stood frozen in rapt attention. No one was shouting any orders, but she noticed a few of the soldiers start to twitch and grab at their heads. One threw off his helmet and vomited; another screamed and started pressing her palms to her temples.

Enacters, she realized. *Even hearing this is hurting them. No, wait. That's not right. An enacter can't be hurt for something someone else does, so if they're in so much pain...they* believe *it. And that decision to believe...*

"Shut this off!" she screamed at no one in particular. "Can't you see it's killing them?!"

Shaking her head, she ran out the door and sprinted to the command center.

THIRTY-SIX
TREASON
COLONEL SAM KILGORE, FCA

Their message delivered and set to play on a loop, Kilgore led the way as his team of special operators, plus Feng and Wang, hurried to the edge of the camp. They were relatively calm, but the colonel was wary as he saw more and more guardmembers around him overcoming their panic and confusion; some were starting to mount a credible defense against the rest of Kilgore's detachment attacking the edges of the Guard base.

Except that not all of them were fighting back. Several were running not outward toward the main attacking force but inward toward the center of the camp. And some were just stopping in their tracks and grabbing at their heads in obvious pain. *What's happening to them?*

"You, stop!" a loud voice called from behind them, and a shot rang out. Kilgore pushed Xin Wang to the ground while Sergeant Lorre did the same with Feng Chu Hua. The operators behind them spun to engage the shooter, except for Corporal Tandy, who had fallen to the ground, either dead or severely wounded from the shot they'd heard.

Blast! the colonel thought as his men took out the small Guard contingent who had raced up behind them and shot Tandy. Whether they had shot him by accident or because they already knew he wasn't a real guardsman was now irrelevant. *They're onto us.*

The exchange of fire had drawn a lot of attention, and several of the rushing guardmembers around them stopped and drew their weapons.

We're in it now, Kilgore thought, raising his own sidearm to fire back.

General James Ostertag, GPF

"Sir, we have reports that elements of the fleet in orbit are refusing orders to launch assault shuttles to support us!"

The voice of his comm officer in the command center jolted General Ostertag from his shock at the message transmitting from the PA speakers.

"Wha—" he started to ask but was interrupted when the door to the building slammed open. Turning, he half-expected to see one of the rebel attackers but was surprised to see a Guard captain, one of the regs, holding a gun pointed at him.

"Captain Portenoy!" cried General Nissen, who had joined Ostertag in the command center shortly after the attack had begun. "What are you doing?"

"Shut up, General!" Kimberly yelled back as several more guardmembers with their weapons also drawn entered the space behind her. "We're here to arrest both of you on charges of dereliction of duty and war crimes against the people of Panamar. We are here to escort you to the stockade pending trial."

"B-but, we're under attack!" sputtered Ostertag, his mind refusing to register what the strange captain had told him

"I know, sir," Portenoy said with false sympathy. "I'll be taking over command of our defenses from here on out. I'm sure I can continue your fine work while these men take you to your new quarters."

Suddenly, Major Rodriguez, standing near Ostertag, drew her

sidearm and pointed it straight at Portenoy's head. "Drop it, Captain," the woman demanded. "Or I drop you."

The captain opened her mouth to respond, but as if on cue, the command center's other door burst open, and Ostertag looked over to see another familiar face brandishing a pistol, a small crowd entering behind him.

"Bohdi?" Captain Portenoy cried in surprise.

The newcomer took in the room with a single sweep of his eyes and kept his pistol pointed at no one in particular.

"Captain Patel, thank goodness you're here! Please take Captain Portenoy into custody and put her and her companions in the stockade," ordered Major Rodriguez as Ostertag and Nissen just stood there dumbly.

Patel shook his head and leveled his pistol at the woman's head from across the room. "Not this time, Tiff," he said, his voice tinged with a deep sadness. "It's over. I won't be party to any more dead children."

The major's mouth dropped.

"I demand you all leave at once!" yelled General Ostertag, regaining his wits. "This is treason, and I will see you all shot—umph!"

He grunted as one of the men who had entered with Bohdi shoved him to his knees and placed his pistol on the back of the old general's head.

"Come on, Tiff, put the gun down," Patel pleaded with Rodriguez, whose aim had never wavered off of Kim Portenoy's head. "These men have broken the very laws we're supposed to enforce, all in the name of following orders. We can be better than this, so much better."

"Bohdi, don't," the woman begged, tears coming to her eyes. "Don't do this. Help me take in these mutineers, and I'll make sure you're rewarded for it. We can forget what happened at the favelas."

"No. We can't." Bohdi's reply was simple, but his voice was firm. "We can't *ever* forget. I don't want to."

He walked slowly across the room, putting his pistol back in the holster on his belt and raising his hands where everyone could see them. He came right up to the trembling major and reached up slowly toward the gun in her hand.

"Don't!" she yelled, taking a step back. "You can't! It's treason!"

Bohdi shook his head sadly and stepped forward again, reaching for the gun once more. This time, the woman didn't move but let him gently take it from her outstretched hand. She was sobbing now, and he put his other arm around her and pulled her into him.

He looked over at Portenoy. "Looks like you're in charge now, Kim. What are your orders?"

Kim shook her head in dumbstruck amazement in the suddenly quiet room. Then she shook herself out of it and started issuing orders as her underlings and Bohdi's took over every station in the command center. All General Ostertag could do was watch impotently.

Sub-Commander Rory Lang, GSF

"Sir! *Raptor* is firing on us! They're demanding we heave to and prepare to be boarded!" the comm officer on the bridge of the Solstice screamed as the ship shook from the impacts of its sister's lasers.

Sub-Commander Rory Lang, previously the ship's chief engineer but now ranking officer with the captain dead and the XO passed out and on his way to sickbay, looked over at the weapons officer for guidance. He had purposefully avoided the command track in the Guard Space Force, mostly because he had always felt unequal to situations exactly like the one he found himself in now.

The weapons officer, a senior lieutenant, must have seen the panic on his superior's face because he didn't wait for orders. "Shields up. Returning fire!"

Colonel Sam Kilgore, FCA

Colonel Kilgore swore as his last pistol clip ran dry. He and the remaining members of his team, now just four surviving operators, an injured Xin, and a frightened Feng had holed up in an empty barracks building and were hunkered down between thin bunks in the center of the room, desperately trying to defend the doors at both ends from about two dozen guardmembers who were just as desperately trying to kill them.

"I'm out!" he shouted.

Next to him, Master Sergeant Lorre grunted. "I'm on my last clip, sir. I think this may be it. There are no other units close enough to get to us in time."

Kilgore couldn't argue with his subordinate's grim assessment. But he was about to try to say something intelligent or reassuring when his thoughts were interrupted by the sound of a new voice from the barrack's loudspeakers.

"Cease fire. All Guard cease fire! Command authentication code Delta Delta Four Six Niner Alpha. Repeat. All Guard cease fire!"

The shooting outside gradually slowed and then stopped. Kilgore's team stopped firing as well—they were almost all out of ammo anyway—and looked to him for orders in the eerie silence.

The voice on the speakers spoke again. Now that he could hear it better and had overcome his initial shock, he registered that it was a woman's voice. "To the rebel soldiers in the camp, we are offering a temporary ceasefire. And I request the company of your commanding officer for a conference in the command center. I will guarantee your safety, but bring as many troops as you'd like."

Kilgore's eyes widened, and he looked over to Lorre as if to get confirmation from the man that he had heard the woman's offer as well. The master sergeant shrugged. "This could be interesting."

Slowly they got to their feet, looking around at the now stilled guardmembers who, only moments before, had been firing at them, and were now milling in a confused fashion around the two entrances.

Suddenly, just as Feng had levered herself up to her feet, a man's voice shouted: "It's the traitor!" Kilgore whirled to see a young guardsman leaping forward toward the diminutive former mech driver and raising his weapon. Kilgore and Xin simultaneously leapt toward Feng to shield her, but it was clear they would both be an instant too late.

A shot echoed in the small room, and Kilgore looked at Feng, expecting to see her crumple to the ground. But instead, she stood still with wide eyes, and he followed her gaze back to the man who had been pointing his gun at her. That guardsman was on the floor, clutching a bullet wound in his shoulder, his own pistol having slid from his grasp and out of his reach.

Behind him, a short man wearing the bodysuit of a mech driver stood with a raised rifle.

"Harrison?!" cried Feng Chu Hua, and before Kilgore could stop her, she rushed to embrace the man who had just saved her life.

But the embrace quickly changed to something else as the young man crumpled and cried out in pain, Feng now fighting to keep him from slamming to the ground.

"Someone help him! Morphine! He needs morphine!" Feng cried out, and a guardswoman came forward and applied a patch to the young man's neck as he now lay writhing on the ground in pain.

He's another enacter, Kilgore realized with astonishment. *He disobeyed his standing orders and shot another guardsman to save Feng!* And any remaining doubts he had had about the mission were suddenly gone.

Sub-Commander Rory Lang, GSF

"The *Raptor* has breached our shields, sir! We can't take much more of this damage!" the weapons officer yelled, trying to get through to the still near-catatonic Sub-Commander Lang.

"Message from the *Firebrand*: they're moving to assist us!" cried the comm officer.

The weapons officer spared a look at the broader battle holo in front of him and saw the other Guard cruiser moving to interpose itself between the *Solstice* and the *Raptor*. In shock, he also saw the entire Guard fleet had broken into pitched battles between isolated ships and small groups. It was utter chaos.

Then he saw something on the edge of the holo field that made his heart drop.

"Detecting a fleet surfacing!" called the sensor officer. "Configurations don't match the Guard. I would say that they're a merchant fleet, but I'm reading heavy weapons signatures and multiple fighter launches.

"Sir!" he looked up, not at Lang, but at the weapons officer. "I think this might be the rebel fleet!"

PART FIVE
AFTERMATH

THIRTY-SEVEN
ADMIRAL
ADMIRAL GERALD WILLIAMS, FCN

Gerald Williams sat in a surprisingly comfortable chair in a small conference room that was attached to the command center structure of the Guard Panamar Expeditionary force's forward operating base. He still couldn't believe how and why he was here.

He looked at the other people in the room. Juan Bolivar was there, of course. He had come huffing into the camp with a contingent of men just hours after the Guard had surrendered and had immediately started taking credit for the entire operation. Xin Wang had tried to pull Williams aside when he'd landed on the planet, but Gerald didn't need Xin to tell him that Bolivar's tenure as rebel commander had been a total disaster. The evidence was there if nowhere else than in the semi-hostile glances he got from even his own men and women.

Xin himself was also in the room, nursing an injured arm, along with the ever-present former Guard Private Feng Chu Hua, who had no real business being there but staunchly refused to leave Xin's side.

Rounding out the rebels in the room was Colonel Sam Kilgore, who, as far as Williams was concerned, would quickly be replacing Bolivar as commander of what was left of the rebel ground forces on the planet.

Then, there were the guardmembers in the room. Captains

Kimberly Portenoy and Bohdi Patel, both non-enacters. Aside from Feng, there were no other enacters or mech officers present, but even they had followed the orders to stop attacking the rebels when no one counteracted Portenoy's original order—complete with Council authorization codes she'd somehow gotten her hands on—to cease fire.

There were other, more senior Guard officers who had enthusiastically supported the ceasefire, but they all seemed content to let Portenoy and Patel run the show, and Gerald was fine with that. Portenoy clearly had some unresolved anger issues toward the mech drivers but was otherwise steady. And Patel had a leadership quality to him that immediately made Williams think he should be much more than a mere captain. Even though Portenoy was the titular head of the traitorous Guard contingent, even she naturally deferred to Patel's judgment on a variety of issues.

"We must fold the Guard traitors into our existing command structure," Bolivar was saying with plenty of bluster, and Gerald could see the looks of shock on the faces of just about everyone else in the room.

"There is simply no other way—" the man continued until Williams put up a hand.

"Juan, stop." Bolivar gave him a look of surprised indignation, but Williams took the sting out of the words. "I'm sure we'll get that all figured out later, but for now, there are more urgent matters that need our collective attention." The man settled down a bit at those words.

"Now," Williams said, turning to look at Portenoy and Patel, "just how many of the Guard have expressed any sort of desire to do the right thing and lay down arms?" Unlike Bolivar, he purposefully avoided the use of the word 'traitors', having seen both Guard officers bristle at the man's earlier use of it.

Portenoy looked over at Bohdi Patel. The young man frowned and pulled up his watch holo. "Unofficially, because I'm not even sure how to go about this officially, roughly a third of the regulars are fed up with the way this war is being run and want nothing more to do with the Guard or its war crimes. I'd guess the number would be much higher, but a lot of these folks have families back home, and they're justifiably worried how the Guard and the Council would react to their defections. But only about a tenth of the total reg forces are still fighting against us in isolated pockets.

"Now," he frowned more deeply. "The mech drivers are an entirely different matter. As you know, all of them, including their support staff and officers, are enacters. None of us regs were allowed anywhere near the mechs."

Williams nodded but stayed silent, intent on letting the man finish, but Bolivar had no such inhibitions.

"So, we should assume that none of them will betray the Guard." the man said, with a finality in his voice that he was obviously sure would be the last word on the matter.

"Actually, no," Bohdi responded, throwing a dark look at the man. "About a tenth of the mech drivers have indicated that they will follow Kim's orders. Most of those are already passed out under heavy doses of morphine, but apparently, seeing Feng and Walker do it and hearing about Nowak was enough to convince them to risk the agony. We have the medics closely monitoring them."

Williams heard Feng gasp in surprise but kept his eyes on Bohdi, who continued talking.

"The rest of the mech drivers fall into two camps. Almost none of them will disobey Kim's ceasefire order since she delivered it with the Council authorization code that that idiot Ostertag left written on his pad so he didn't have to memorize it. But about a quarter of them are outright hostile and would be attacking us now if they had the courage to break their orders. A few tried, in fact, but we got the mechs locked down pretty quickly, and their erstwhile drivers are now occupying the various stockades.

"And the remaining ones, they're pretty much neutral. They won't stay here and follow us unless they get another official order to do so, but they have accepted Kim's ceasefire orders for the time being and are waiting to see what happens next. Some of them have light headaches from the contradictions they're trying to reconcile in their heads, but most are just acting as if it's business as usual and seem to be doing OK."

Williams shook his head in amazement. "That's incredible," he said. "And to think that all it took was an exceptionally-crafted broadcast."

"Why, yes, and Colonel Kilgore, acting under my orders, did his job very well," Bolivar said smugly from the other end of the table.

Williams felt anger flash through him and knew he should moderate his words, but decided it just wasn't worth it anymore. "Shut up, Juan," he said calmly, so calmly that the General did a literal double-take, wondering if he'd heard his commanding officer correctly. "Let's just say," Williams continued, "that I know what roles everyone played in what happened here today, and you are in this room only out of respect for your rank and what good you did here commanding the rebel forces up until today."

Everyone tried but failed not to look at Bolivar to see his reaction. The short general had a look of complete shock on his face, and his mouth moved open and closed as if trying to get words out, but none would come.

"General Bolivar," Williams said, his tone still gentle but firm, brooking no argument. "I will not let your good deeds be overlooked, but I am ordering you to leave the room for now. You are relieved of command."

For a moment, it looked as if Juan Bolivar would argue—like he would yell at the legendary Admiral Ironsides, who had led the rebellion's hidden military operations for the last decade. But instead, he slowly got up from his seat and actually left the room.

There were palpable sighs of relief around the table as the door shut behind the general, but Williams ignored them and turned back to Portenoy and Patel. "Now, where were we? Oh yes, let's talk about the disposition of the Guard ships still in orbit."

THIRTY-EIGHT
REBEL
EX-CAPTAIN BOHDI PATEL, GPF DESERTER

"Why would you want to stay here?" Bohdi asked the rebel officer he'd just met a few hours before.

Colonel Sam Kilgore looked at him with an amused expression. "Well, it's home."

Bohdi shook his head. "Look, I'm as fond of where I grew up as much as the next guy, but this has got to be the worst planet I've ever been on. Everything here wants to kill you, and I swear I saw a mosquito fly off carrying one of the mechs yesterday."

Kilgore threw back his head and laughed. The two officers had found that they were kindred spirits and were taking a stroll around the Guard's forward operating base, both trailed by nervous attendants and self-appointed bodyguards at a distance.

"Well," Kilgore said, letting out a loud breath through his nose, "I've been fighting the Council on Panamar for so long that I guess I'm just not ready to give it up. Leaving feels like quitting, and I have family here, as do most of my troops."

"But you'll be back to fighting a lone and losing guerrilla war," Bohdi argued, though he knew he wasn't going to convince the man.

"That's right, and we know how to do that," Kilgore replied. "But more importantly, we can now do so with real hope. Hope that we might actually win and make a difference."

"Like you did here today," Bohdi said.

Kilgore grinned at him and pulled out one of the horrid-smelling cigars he seemed to favor, sticking it in the side of his mouth and lighting it as he lightly chuckled around it. "Well," he said once he had it lit, "what happened here today was supposed to be a suicide mission. And it would have been without you and Portenoy and the troops loyal to both of you. And I have to believe there are other good people in the Guard like the two of you and that maybe we'll run into some more of them when the next Guard fleet comes to put us down."

Bohdi smiled lightly, taking the man's praise for what it was and knowing it was sincere.

"Now," Kilgore asked between puffs on the cigar, "what's going to happen to that major of yours?"

Bohdi didn't have to ask who he was referring to. "Tiff just isn't ready to turn rebel," he said, trying but failing to keep the sadness out of his voice. "She's agreed to take command of the Guard that are choosing to head back to Greater York—basically everyone who doesn't want to join the rebellion—but she's going to go back and face the music for her actions here. And knowing how the Guard works, Ostertag and Nissen will probably both throw her under the bus to the first Planetary Commissioner or Prefect who will listen to them."

Kilgore shook his head. "I'm sorry. It's hard to see someone you care about making a decision like that, especially when you know they're doing it all for the right reasons. Still, maybe the recordings of the atrocities the enacters were committing will help sway some folks in her favor."

Bohdi shook his head. "Problem is that anyone that senior is an enacter with decades of loyal Council service, and we can't count on them to disobey their orders like a few did here. Also, I've noticed that the only enacters who are disobeying orders seem to be fairly young, all under the age of forty and most under the age of thirty. Not sure if there's a pattern there or not, but the older ones seem to be immune from whatever is allowing the others to disobey."

Kilgore grunted thoughtfully but made no other response. They walked in silence for a few minutes as Bohdi ruminated sadly on losing Tiff from his life. They'd only been together a few months, but it had seemed like it had a chance to go somewhere when Bohdi eventually got promoted, and they didn't have to sneak around anymore. *Then again,* he thought, *the sneaking around was always Tiff's favorite part. Maybe she would have lost interest once we could have become official.*

He shook off the thought just as Kilgore spoke again. "How about you? You're sure about things?"

Bohdi nodded without hesitation. This topic didn't require nearly as much thought as it probably should have. "No question. After seeing what the Guard leadership was capable of doing here in San Sebastian, I have no desire to ever be part of their ranks again. And aside from my parents and sister, I have no family to leave behind. Besides, I really think my mom and dad would understand and even approve of what I'm doing. Either way, my career with the Guard is over, and I guess I'm a rebel now."

Kilgore nodded. "Well, we're mighty glad to have you. If I'm reading things right, I think your promotion to a higher rank will be pretty quick. Williams seems to respect you, and I've seen how the troops in this camp regard you and follow your lead."

Bohdi said nothing in reply. Nothing he could say wouldn't sound like bragging or false modesty.

"Take my advice," Kilgore said, stopping and turning to face him. "Stick close to Admiral Williams. That man has a plan in his head for how this is all going to end, even if he's not sharing it now. A big part of me wants to leave Panamar just to go with him, but I have ties here that are too strong. But you have an opportunity to go along with him and do great things. Maybe, who knows, you'll even be part of the final push against the Council one of these days."

Bohdi nodded. Again, he said nothing. There was nothing he felt he could add to that.

EPILOGUE
LIEUTENANT FENG CHU HUA, FCN

THREE MONTHS LATER – 731 P.D.

Feng Chu Hua smiled as an arm wrapped itself around her waist from behind, and she felt the warm touch of lips on her ear.

"You're distracting me again," she said wryly, turning to look up at the grinning face of newly-promoted Commander Xin Wang.

"A fighter pilot has to learn to deal with all sorts of distractions," he said playfully while reaching up with his free hand to start massaging her neck.

She squirmed enough to break his grip and then *tried* to get back to reading the space fighter specs sheet in the holo in front of her.

"Besides," Xin said from behind her, "your simulations have been going great. You're a natural in the cockpit of a fighter, just like you were in a mech."

She rolled her eyes and shook her head, though he could only see the latter. "Being good in sims doesn't always translate to real life," she chided him. "Sarah taught me that. It only took her about a week to show me that being hot stuff in my old training mech didn't even translate to the same in my combat suit. It took me months of hard drilling to get even halfway as comfortable in the combat rig."

She turned and looked back and up at him, resisting the urge to roll her eyes again at the stupid grin on his face. "I've got my first real solo flight tomorrow, and I have to pass it so that Commander Horton will let me keep going in my training. And *you're* going to make me fail."

Xin grinned widely and shrugged. "Actually, the best thing I think you can do before a test is clear your mind a bit with something… highly distracting."

A second later, she was standing up and kissing him, all arguments gone.

Even with Xin's near-constant distractions, it only took Feng Chu Hua two more months to earn her wings and to take her place in the Free Colonies Navy as one of its newest fighter pilots. And with that, she finally felt that she was doing something that truly mattered.

THE END

Don't ever miss a new release!

Sign up now for Skyler's newsletter and get access to new release updates, free content, and great deals.

Just go to www.skylerramirez.com/join-the-club

BOOKS BY SKYLER RAMIREZ

DUMB LUCK AND DEAD HEROES

The Worst Ship in the Fleet
The Worst Spies in the Sector
The Worst Pirate Hunters in the Fringe
The Worst Rescuers in the Republic
The Worst Detectives in the Federation
The Worst Traitors in the Confederacy
The Worst Fugitives in the Star Nation
The Worst Mercenaries in the Border Systems (Coming Soon)

A STAR NATION IN PERIL

Set in the same universe as Dumb Luck and Dead Heroes

Rogue Agent

Suicide Mission

Assassin's Flight (Coming Soon)

THE BRAD MENDOZA CHRONICLES

Set in the same universe as Dumb Luck and Dead Heroes

Saving the Academy

Battle for Poe

Siege of Jalisco

THE FOUR WORLDS

The Four Worlds: The Truth

The Four Worlds: Subversion

The Four Worlds: Wrath of Mars (Coming Soon)

Revolution: A Four Worlds Story

ANTHOLOGIES

AI Apocalypse: A Collection of Science Fiction Stories (with Jonathan Yanez, Andrew Moriarty, Anthony J Melchiorri, and Stephen Gay)

ABOUT THE AUTHOR

I just love writing. It's as simple as that. My goal is to write books that my readers enjoy and that celebrate everyday imperfect heroes. I want to show that everyone, no matter how life has dealt with them or how they've dealt with life, deserves a second chance and can go on to do amazing things. Just look at Brad and Jessica in Dumb Luck and Dead Heroes or Jinny Ambrosa and Tyrus Tyne in The Four Worlds.

It's important to me that everyone be able to read my books, including my teenage children, so I purposefully leave out any swearing or graphic scenes. In this, I follow a tradition set by many (far better) writers before me, most notably in my life, Louis L'Amour. I can only aspire to write even half as good as Mr. L'Amour!

As for the personal side, I live in Texas with my wife and four children (and often a revolving door of exchange students), and I work for a major tech company for my day job. But writing is my passion, and I often toil into the early hours of morning, especially on the weekends, and it's all worth it when I see people enjoy my books.

Thanks for reading!

Skyler Ramirez

        amazon.com/author/Skyler-Ramirez
        facebook.com/skylerramirezauthor
        instagram.com/skyler.ramirez.author
        tiktok.com/@skylerramirez_author

Printed in Dunstable, United Kingdom